'...sta by his furry shorts!'

KT-432-896

The Confessions of Georgia Nicolson:

Angus, thongs and full-frontal snogging

'It's OK, I'm wearing really big Knickers!'

'Knocked out by my nunga-nungas.'

'Dancing in my nuddy-pants!'

'...and that's when it fell off in my hand.'

'...then he ate my boy entrancers.'

'...startled by his furry shorts!'

'Luuurve is a many trousered thing...'

Also available on tape and CD:

'...and that's when it fell off in my hand.'

'...then he ate my boy entrancers.'

'...startled by his furry shorts!'

'Luuurve is a many trousered thing...'

'...startled by his furry shorts!'

Louise Rennison

HarperCollins *Children's Books*

This edition produced for The Book People Ltd,
Hall Wood Avenue, Haydock, St Helens, WA11 9UL

Find out more about Georgia at www.georgianicolson.com

First published in Great Britain in hardback by HarperCollins Children's Books in 2006
First published in Great Britain in paperback by HarperCollins Children's Books in 2007
HarperCollins Children's Books is a division of HarperCollinsPublishers Ltd,
77-85 Fulham Palace Road, Hammersmith, London W6 8JB

www.harpercollinschildrensbooks.co.uk

1

ISBN 978-0-00-782479-3

Printed and bound in England by
Clays Ltd, St Ives plc

Mixed Sources
Product group from well-managed
forests and other controlled sources
www.fsc.org Cert no. SW-COC-1806
© 1996 Forest Stewardship Council

FSC is a non-profit international organisation established to promote the
responsible management of the world's forests. Products carrying the FSC
label are independently certified to assure consumers that they come
from forests that are managed to meet the social, economic and
ecological needs of present and future generations.

Find out more about HarperCollins and the environment at
www.harpercollins.co.uk/green

In memory and love of Dezza the Vicar.

Big luuurve to my family and friends, old and new. (Look, I'm not saying some of you are old, I'm just saying that some of you are newer than others... er... but not in a less old way. Oh, look, I just love you, right?)

Enormous panty-splitting thanks to my editors and publicists and designers and sales people at HarperCollins in Billy Shakespeare land and Hamburger-a-gogo land.

Thanks as always to the Empress.

But mostly thank you to my lovely, lovely readers (which now even include some vatis, which is a bit alarming).

A Note from Georgia

Dear worldwide Chums and Chumettes,

(Hang on a minute, when I say "worldwide" I don't mean "enormously fat", I merely mean internationalwise.) Where was I before you got the wrong end of the stick? Oh yes, do you know how much I love you all? A LOT. That is how much. I do, it is *le* fact. Why else would I spend so much time rifling through my creative drawers (oo-er) writing another diary?

Actually, as I say to anyone who will listen (i.e., no one), I am practically a saint in human form. But there's very little thanks in it. For instance, the other day I helped a little old lady across the road. I didn't have to. In fact, I was in a tearing dash on my way to get new lip gloss. But I did, and do you know what she did? She hit me with her umbrella! She said she didn't want to cross the road, she was waiting for her friend to pick her up to go pole dancing!!!

That is the kind of world we live in.

The elderly insane, like Elvis Attwood, parents, etc., say that young people only care about lipstick and snogging. I say hahahaha. If they would take the trouble to read works of geniosity like mine, they would soon realise that we do many useful and creative things. Who invented the terms "piddly-diddly department" and "poo-parlour division" that are used in schools all over the world? Before I bothered to invent "nunga-nungas", what fools we felt calling our breasty substances, er... breasts.

Do you see?

I think you do.

Goodbye and God bless you all.

And also S'laters.

Georgia

p.s. And I invented nervy b. and f.t. and so on.

p.p.s. And the Viking disco inferno dance.

p.p.p.s. I could go on but I feel slightly tired with creativitosity and I may... zzzzzzzzzzzzzzzzzzzzzzzzz.

Living in Fiasco land

Saturday June 18th
9:00 p.m.

I can't believe I am once more on the rack of romance.

And also in the oven of luuurve.

And possibly on my way to the bakery of pain.

And maybe even going to stop along the way to get a little cake at the cake shop of agony.

Shut up, brain. Shut up.

Looking out of my bedroom window at the stars
9:01 p.m.

It says in my *Meditation for the Very Backward* book that it is soothing looking at the universe and stars and everything.

Ommmm.

9:03 p.m.

The meditation book is wrong. God, stars are annoying. Winking and blinking like twinkly idiots. Why are they so cheerful?

9:03 p.m. and a half

I'll tell you why they are so cheerful: because they are not me. They know nothing of the call of the Horn and snogging. Has a Luuurve God ever said to one of them, "I will let you know in a week's time if I want to go out with you or not"? No.

Anyway, what are stars for actually? You can't even read by them. They just hang about. Like dim torches.

9:04 p.m.

Hanging about is not exactly a job, is it?

9:05 p.m.

I am not as such feeling any calmer.

9:10 p.m.

Being in the bakery of pain is vair vair boring. Ten past nine on a Saturday night and I am in my bedroom. Alone. I am in the prime of my – er – hornosity and *joie de vivre* and nothing is going on. Nothing.

It's like a grave in this house. I...

Oh good, my darling little sister has kicked open my door and flung my cat Angus at me.

"HEGGGGOOO, Gingey!!! We is back. Heggo!!! Watch my panties dance. Sex bum, sex bum, am a sex bum!!!"

Oh dear *Gott* in *Himmel*. Angus was livid at being thrown, and once he'd stopped doing that cat sneezing and shaking thing he dug his claws into my ankle. Owwwwwww. Now I'm on the way to the cake shop of aggers with a gammy leg. Hurray!

Libby put her frock over her head and waggled her botty around like a pole dancer. Where does she see people doing these things?

They've just come back from the lunatic asylum, i.e., Grandad's sheltered housing, so it will be something she has seen there. I've seen the residents in their so-called communal lounge. They pretend to play dominoes, but secretly they practise being mad. And probably prance around in their incontinence knickers.

Then Mum came mumming in and scooped up Bibbs. "Time for Boboland, young lady."

Libby carried on singing and wiggling around in Mum's arms, and then Mum noticed me. Being in my bedroom.

"What are you up to, Georgia? Why are you in here?"

I said, "Not that anyone notices, but this is actually my room. You know, for me to be in. I was in bed, as it happens."

Mum said as she went out, "Oh, you must be sooo tired, all that lip gloss and mascara to carry round all day."

Vair vair amusing. Not.

9:25 p.m.

I've been in my bedroom for more or less twenty-four hours, give or take snack and loo breaks. Oh, and a quick visit to the shops for essentials. Mascara and a new nunga-nunga holder. And a copy of *Cosmo*. It is more than twenty-four hours since Masimo left me at my door saying he would let me know if he wanted me to be his girlfriend or not. Why did I admit I wanted him to be like my proper boyfriend? Why why?

9:26 p.m.

And also thrice why? Why why why? Why couldn't I have just been a callous sophisticate? I could for once have just shut up and been all full of casualosity and *savoir* whatsit.

9:30 p.m.

If I'd played my cards right I could have had loads of boyfriends. All at the same time. Masimo the Italian Stallion for a weekendy boyfriend, with a touch of Dave the Laugh (oo-er) for a rainy weekday. And also maybe even the former Sex God (whose name I'm not going to mention even beyond the grave) as a sort of Kiwi-a-gogo airmail boyfriend. But, oh no, I had to moan on about wanting to be Masimo's one and only.

9:40 p.m.

I was so happy snogging Masimo under the stars on our date. Stars didn't get on my nerves then. Nothing did.

9:42 p.m.

How come I am living in Fiasco land again? One minute he was snogging me under the twinkly twits, and then the next he is off to Late and Live with Wet Lindsay, stick insect and drip.

I am haunted by old Droopy Drawers. First she enticed you know who, whose name I will never mention even beyond the grave, but as a clue his name starts with "R" and ends in "obbie". Now she has slimed her way around Masimo. I hate her, I hate her.

But that is life in a nutshell, isn't it? Well, mine anyway – all fabby and marvy and then all pooey and *merde*.

9:45 p.m.

What was it Charlie Dickens said in his famous book *Oliver Twit*? Ah, yes, "Forsooth and lack a day all ye worlde is-eth a stage and verily we-eth are players in-eth it. Gadzooks." Or was that Billy Shakespeare?

Who knows? Who cares? What does it mean, anyway? And why do none of those beardy Elizabethan types know how to speak proper English?

What does anything mean?

Midnight

Oh, I can't bear this. How many hours will it be until

Masimo tells me his answer? Perhaps I should phone him and tell him that I didn't mean what I said about him being my one and only one. I could say that he can go out with Wet Lindsay as well, as long as he likes me too.

12:10 a.m.
But then I might snog him after she has snogged him, and that would mean I have practically snogged her. No one could live with that.

12:20 a.m.
I would rather snog Angus.

12:26 a.m.
I bet Angus is a much better snogger than her.
   Much better.

12:30 a.m.
He has certainly got nicer legs.

12:31 a.m.
Well, more of them, anyway.

12:36 a.m.

Everyone has gone to bed. And the kittykats are out. I can hear them yowling and spitting in the garden somewhere. Cross-eyed Gordy is practically a teenager in cat years now. I'll bet he is doing keepie-uppie like Oscar, the so-called son of Mr and Mrs Across the Road, otherwise known as Perv Boy. No, what I mean is, he will be pretending to do keepie-uppie but really keeping his eyes out for female-type kittykats.

12:39 a.m.

Actually, Gordy would be much better at keepie-uppie and girl spotting than Oscar because he could quite literally do them at the same time – keep one eye on the ball and use the other one for spotting girly kittykats. His spaggy eye would be a blessing in disguise.

12:41 a.m.

Oooh, I can't sleep. I must read a book of wisdomosity.

12:42 a.m.

It says in my (well, officially Mum's) book *How to Make Any*

Twit Fall in Love with You that if you pretend to feel how you feel, then you will feel like you feel.

Pardon?

12:45 a.m.

For instance, it says, "If you go to a party and you feel shy, enter the room with a wide smile. Put your shoulders back, hold your head high, let your arms hang loosely by your side. Then, even if you don't feel confident, no one will ever know!"

Okey dokey, I'll try that in the mirror.

Wide smile, arms loosey loose and swing. Big smile, shoulders back, head high, swing swing. Loosey loose arms and swing swing.

12:52 a.m.

Yep, I definitely look confident. There is one tiny drawback, though: hanging my arms loosely and swinging them makes me look like an orang-utan. An orang-utan called Ralf, probably. And who wants a confident orang-utan as a girlfriend? That is what I ask myself.

♡ 17

12:54 a.m.

Ralf the confident orang-utan wearing Teletubbies pyjamas. Which I only wore for comfortnosity. I had no idea I was going to have to go out to a party in them looking confident.

Shut up, brain.

Sunday June 19th
My bedroom
10:00 a.m.

Same rack of love.

Same oven of pain.

Same bakery of... shutup shutup.

I would usually consult with Dave the Laugh about the Luuurve God scenario. He is after all the official Hornmeister and Pants King. It still makes me laugh like a drain when I think of him singing, "The hills are alive with the sound of pants!" I would ask him to give me the benefit of his wisdomosity about boys and so on, but he's gone a bit weird with all that "What if we should have really been together?" fandango, so I feel a bit funny about seeing him again.

11:00 a.m.

Mutti popped her head round my door. "We're going to Waterworld. Do you want to come?"

I said, "Are you mad?"

I said it in a polite and inquiring way, but she still went ballisticisimus. "You are so bloody rude."

I very nearly said that swearing shows a lack of vocabulary, but I didn't because I am so vair vair tired.

11:30 a.m.

The Swiss Family Mad have "roared" off in the clown car – otherwise known as Dad's ludicrous three-wheeled Robin Reliant – leaving me alone at Château Sheer Desperadoes.

11:35 a.m.

I'm going mad. I am going to have to phone The Big Knickered One, and hope she doesn't ramble on about bat droppings.

Phoned Jas.

Jas was so much in Jas 'n' Tom land that she didn't even notice I was in the bakery of pain. She just went on rambling for Europe. "Oooh, it's so groovy that Tom's back!

♥

I only saw him briefly yesterday. He is going to bring around his flora collection from Kiwi-a-gogo land in a bit and that will be soo... oh..."

I said, "Indescribably dull?"

She said, "I have to go now."

"Jazzy Wazzy, can I come and see you? I need your help."

"No."

Jas's bedroom
Lunchtime

I am lying amongst Jas's sad collection of stuffed toys, mostly owls, while she ponces around in front of a mirror. What is she doing?

I said, "Jas it's very distracting trying to tell you stuff, important stuff full of tragicosity about me your very bestest pally, when you keep pouting like a goldfish. What are you doing?"

"I'm practising puckering."

"What?"

"Puckering. I had, well, a bit of a problem vis-à-vis snogging with Tom last night."

Despite my world coming apart at the seams, I am always

interested in snogging tales. "Tell me."

"Well, I was quite nervy at first when I was waiting for him."

"Were you doing your annoying flicky-fringe thing?"

"I don't know; anyway, when he came in, I was sort of jelloid. But then it was all right because he got his whatsits out."

"Pardon?"

"His, you know, snapshots from Kiwi-a-gogo land, so we looked at them for a bit. Until I felt calmed down. Actually there was a really cool one of Robbie..."

Oh brilliant. On top of everything else I was now talking about someone I had vowed I would never talk about this side of the grave.

I said, "Was Robbie playing the guitar and dancing with marsupials?"

Jas wasn't even listening. "Anyway, as we were looking at them Tom got closer to me and put his arm around me. Then we, well... we, you know, started snogging and so on."

"And so on? Where is 'and so on' on the snogging scale? What number did you get to?"

"Er... five and a bit of six. It was really groovy. I felt like I was all melting in to him and then... well... then I had sort of a lip spasm."

"A LIP SPASM?"

Ten minutes later

Apparently she had been snogging away when she had suddenly had the lip spaz.

She said, "I got cramp in my lips and they sort of seized up."

"What does that look like?"

And she showed me. Blimey. You know when you put food in a baby's mouth and it doesn't like it, and its eyes go all goggly and then its whole face goes into a spasm and the food comes shooting out of its mouth? Well, even if you don't know, believe me, I do. Libby could make rice pudding reach the other side of the room.

While Jas was showing me her spazzy face, I said, "If you don't mind me saying, Jas, that is not very attractive."

She said, "I expect it was snogging withdrawal. I hadn't puckered up for ages, so... you know, being out of practice... but it won't happen again."

"Good."

"Because I have an exercise regime now. Shall I show you?

"No."

"OK. It goes pucker, relax, pucker, relax, pucker, relax. Do you see?"

I didn't say anything, just lay there staring at her with big starey eyes like the rest of the owls as she pouted her lips and then relaxed them. She looked like a mixture of Mick Jagger and an idiot. Not necessarily in that order.

She was in full ramble mode now. "And then for the *pièce de résistance* it's darty tongue, darty tongue."

God, it was horrible sitting there while her little tongue went in and out like a mad vole. Fortunately I was able to shove a Midget Gem in her gob so that I could tell her the sad tale of my Italian Stallion.

Ten minutes later

She said (chewy chew), "So you said that he had to be your one and only boyfriend scenario or else that was it? *Arrivederci*, Masimo?"

I said, "Yes, but..."

"Well, what in the name of Slim's outsize pyjamas were

♡ 23

you thinking of? Are you mad?"

"No, I'm not mad, Jas. I just happen to have a friend who looks a lot like you who said, 'Just be yourself.'"

"What?"

"You said being yourself and genuine was like having a generous nose. Like I have got. The exact words used were: 'Just because you have a generous nose, don't go to the nose-disguiser shop; let your own nose run free and wild.'"

"What complete fool said that?"

"YOU did, Jas."

"Did I? Well, yeah, but I didn't mean it, did I? Clearly. That was in the sanctity of our own brains, wasn't it? I mean, we were going to the PRETEND nose-disguiser shop. I didn't actually mean you should BE yourself. That is just stupid."

I really really could kill her. In fact, if I attacked her stupid fringe suddenly, she might choke on her stupid Midget Gem, and that would be good.

Sadly, Jas had got interested now. She said, "So let me get this right – he's choosing between you and Wet Lindsay? Blimey, does she know that? Because if she does, you are dead as a doughnut. Deader."

Cheers.

The doorbell rang downstairs, and a minute later Tom bounded into the room. He said, "Hey, Georgia... gidday, as our Kiwi pals say! Bonzer to see you!" And he gave me a big, proper boy hug. It felt really nice. Especially as I may never feel another boy's jumper next to my head in this lifetime, the way things are going.

He sat down on the bed and looked at both of us and said, "OK, what have you two been talking about? Lipstick?"

We both looked offended. Tom went on, "Erm... world peace, the Manchester United attacking four? Snogging?"

I said with dignitosity at all times, "I've got a lot more on my mind than boys, Tom. There are other things in the world, you know."

He said, "So it's all over with you and the Italian Stallion then?"

"No, well, er maybe... oh, I don't know." And I blurted out the whole story because it was so nice to have a boy type to talk to. And, for a boy, Tom is very nearly not quite completely insane.

At the end he lay back on Jas's stuffed owl family and said, "Wow."

I looked at him.

He looked at me. "Wowzee wow and wow."

Jas said, "I know, that's what I thought."

What are they, the idiot telepathic twins?

I said to Tom, "What do you think?"

He said, "Well, you know he's just come out of a big relationship and, well, he's a fit-looking guy, isn't he? Not that I'm on the turn or anything. But he is. He could pretty much have any chick he wanted."

Jas was nodding away like Tom was Dr Ruth, psychiatrist to the Hollywood set, or something. And she shuffled up really close to him. It's pathetic.

Tom went on talking, "Georgia, you don't think he's, you know, well, a bit worried that you might be a bit... well, unusual?"

I said, "Unusual? Like how?"

Tom said, "Well, when he first asked you if you wanted a drink, you went off disco dancing to Rolf Harris's 'Two Little Boys'."

Oh goddygodgod, am I never to be free from my own bonkerosity?

I said, "What else is a person supposed to do when their

boy entrancers get stuck together?"

Jas was still doing her nodding along wisely fiasco. She said to Tom, "Yes, yes, I see what you mean. He may be afraid to go out with her, and really who can blame him?"

I was just about to lunge for her throat when her mum knocked on the door and said, "May I come in for a moment, Jas? Dad and I are off to the allotment and then we may pop into the club for a quick game of cards, so I've left snacks in the kitchen. I know how you young people eat! Bye."

Her mutti and vati were going to their allotment. Jas's mum was wearing welligogs and a proper mum-sized pair of trousers and a cardi. Her vati probably doesn't even know what leather trousers are. My vati has a clown car and my mum came in last night with her T-shirt on inside out. How am I supposed to know how to behave? Why would any Luuurve God want to have anything to do with me? Oh nooo, please don't let me blub.

Tom looked at me and then he put his arm around me. "Listen, Georgia, if he doesn't get you then its his loss. You're fab; we all know that."

Jas even had a go at being nice. "Yes, you are, er... fab,

and you are so, you know... you. I mean, you wouldn't be you if you weren't you, would you?"

What was she rambling on about?

Tom was fishing about in his rucky. "I've got something to show you, Gee."

Oh blimey, now he was going to get his newts out or something, at a time like this. He handed me a pile of photos. Oh good, they were of his trip to Kiwi-a-gogo land. How interesting. Not.

I flicked through them. Trees, trees, sheep, trees, Kiwi-a-gogo people in big boots and shorts and funny beards. And the men were just as bad!!! Hahahahahaha. Oh, shutup, brain. More sheep, wombat droppings, rogue bores, more beards, sheep, trees, sheep and... then I saw the photo of you know who. The Original Sex God Heartbreaker. Smiling into the camera. With dreamy dark blue eyes. Suntanned. Standing in a river wearing shorts. Thank goodness I had eschewed him with a firm hand and felt nothing.

One minute later
Corrrrrr. And also phwoar.

Back in my bedroom of pain
7:00 p.m.

I felt like a goosegog extraordinaire round at Jazzy Spazzy's. All that hand holding and giggling, it's pathetic. I may as well have been the wife of the Invisible Man. Mrs Invisible Man. It was all kissy kiss kiss, "Oooooohhh, Tom, do you like my new shoes? Oooohhh, Tom, I've got a new owl." Pathetic. I would never do that in front of anyone. I needn't worry, though, because if Masimo chooses Wet Lindsay, I am going to be living in a lesbian monastery for the rest of my life.

Five minutes later

Life really has gone *merde* when I can't even speak to my besty pally because she is so BUSY with her boyfriend.

Well, so be it: if she chooses Tom above me, that is her lookout.

I will be eschewing her with a firm hand.

A LOT.

Like I am eschewing Robbie.

I will not have him in my brain. There is no room for anyone else in the cake shop of agony; it's crowded enough in there already.

And, anyway, Masimo is my one and only one.

Maybe.

Ten minutes later

I hate Jas. My so-called friend and bestie.

But I tell you this for free: she will never know how much she has hurt me. I might be in pain, but at least I have my dignitosity.

That I will never give up for anyone.

One minute later

Phoned Jas.

"Jas, what do you think Masimo will say? Do you think he wants to go out with me? Would you go out with me if you were him?"

"Oy, don't start that lezzie business again."

"Jas, I am just asking you to imagine being him and what you would think about me if you were him. I mean, you wouldn't pick Wet Lindsay over me, would you?"

"She's got quite nice arms."

"Jas, that is the wrong answer. The correct answer is, 'Of course I would choose you every time, Georgia, you gorgey creature.'"

"Well, if you already know the answer, what is the point of asking me the question?"

"And, by the way, what do you mean she has got nice arms? She's a stick insect, therefore she's got sticky thin stupid arms. And unusually enough for a stick insect, it doesn't stop there – she's got a stupid forehead and stupid feet and—"

"I've not seen her feet unclothed. Have you? When did you see her feet?"

"Jas, I don't know that I have seen her feet, but I know that they are sad. Anyway, stop going on and on about her feet. I'm not interested in her bloody feet."

"Well, I didn't start the feet business. I was only being polite."

I slammed down the phone. I may be having a nervy spaz.

I'd better eat something sweet.

In the Kitchen
Nothing to eat, of course.

I must and shall have sugar.

Five minutes later

Never have sugar on bread. It is disgusting.

7:30 p.m.

I had better plan what I'm going to wear the day he comes round to see me. It may be the deciding factor between happinosity and sadnosity.

I must make sure he doesn't see me in my school uniform. It will only remind him that I go to school.

I think I'll practise smiling in the mirror.

7:40 p.m.

Oh, what larks, I'm developing a lurker on my chin. Perfect. It should just be nicely ripening into a massive red pus-filled second chin by Friday.

Five minutes later

Typico, I have run out of spot cream. I could squirt some perfume on it; that sometimes works. What does it say in *CosmoGIRL!* vis-à-vis lurker alerts?

Five minutes later

Apparently you are supposed to lure out the lurker by encouraging it to come to a head. You should steam the area. With a steaming thing.

Ten minutes later

I've had my face over a boiling saucepan for the last year and a half, and although my face is bright red and dripping with water, the lurker is still lurking there happily.

In *Cosmo*'s beauty hints it says you can use a poultice to draw it out. What can I use as a poulticey-type thing? It says a muslin bag with herbs and stuff in it.

In the bathroom

I have just looked in the "medical chest" and it has got some mouldy old oranges, a leg from Libby's Pantalitzer doll, and some dried cat poo in it. How disgusting.

In Mutti and Vati's bedroom

I've found some corn plasters in a drawer. Maybe they would do as a poultice. I'll stick one over the lurker.

One minute later

Well, that is attractive. Not.

But who said that love was painless?

One minute later

And who said it involved corn plasters?

8:10 p.m.

God, the lurker is throbbing. I hope the corn plaster poulticey thing isn't drawing anything else out. I don't want to wake up with no chin.

Wandering lonely as a clud round the house
8:15 p.m.

I may as well be an orphan, for all the notice my family takes of me. They went out gaily laughing and singing years ago, leaving me with a measly fiver for a whole day. Just out scaring people for hours and hours.

I hate them.

It's a bit spooky in the house by myself. Even the kittykats are nowhere around. What if an escaped prisoner came in out of the night and broke into the house to get food and so on?

He wouldn't stay long, I can tell you that.

Ten minutes later
I never thought the day would come when I would be glad to hear the whine of Vati's half-horsepower clown car, but it has.

I scampered up to my bedroom.

Loony alert
One minute later
Bang bang, crash. Why can no one in my family open a door normally? Crashing around when starving people with two chins are trying to sleep.

Mum came upstairs into my room. I don't know why she bothers having her own room.

She sat on the bed and looked at me. What am I? A looking at person?

She said, "Could you tell me why you've got a corn plaster on your chin?"

I said, "Oh, leave me alone, will you?"

"Georgia, what is the matter with you? Seriously, you seem all worried and upset – what is it?"

And then, I don't know what happened, but I told her. "I said to the Italian Stallion that I wanted him to be like my proper boyfriend, and he said, 'Oh, this is a serious thing', you know, in that really groovy accent-type thing, and then Dave the Laugh said, 'What if you really liked someone and then you lost them', and Jas said, 'Wet Lindsay has got nice feet and he might like that'... maybe they do, the Italians, they are an ancient race and maybe they like feet... and then a lurking lurker situation occurred, so I got out the corn plaster... and he's going to choose on Friday, that's five days away... and the *coup de* whatsit is that the Original Sex God, whose name I will never mention this side of the grave, had his shorts on, in a river, probably showing off to his wombat friends... Oh, what is the point?"

Actually, for a complete fool and someone who tosses her nunga-nungas around with gay abandon, Mum was quite nice. And she seemed to understand.

Which I am surprised at, as I don't know what I'm saying myself most of the time.

And I'm in my head. Sadly.

10:00 p.m.

Mum gave me a kiss, and I even let her cuddle me. A bit. She said the corn plaster wouldn't work, but she would get me some cream tomorrow that will dry the lurker up.

She said I should keep myself busy with a list of things to do until Friday so that I don't have time to go mad.

Good idea. I will start on the list now.

Two minutes later

This is my list:

Practise not being mad.

10:35 p.m.

Mum brought Bibbs into bed with me. She was asleep, still clutching her swimming goggles and snorkel. She was also clutching the statue of Our Lord Jesus, or Sandra, as he is now called in his Barbie frock and make-up. He is Libby's new best "fwend". I looked at Bibbs in the half-light in my bedroom. She is so sweet when she is asleep. Her little eyelashes are long and curly and her mouth all pouty and pink. I cuddled up to her, and she turned over in her sleep and put her little arms round me. Oooooohhhhh. I said softly, "Night-night, my little sister. I love you."

And she said sleepily, "Night-night, Ginger. I lobe you."

Ooohhh. At least she loves me.

Then she whispered, "Ginger, I poo my jimjams, oh dear."

Midnight

After emergency removal of my pooey sister, I eventually snuggled down into my bed of pain alone. Not entirely alone because there is a bit of a residual pong and Sandra/Jesus is still in bed with me.

2:00 a.m.

Woke up from a dream.

I dreamt that I had a conversation with Jesus. He had the hump because he didn't like his frock and he said his lipstick didn't suit his complexion. It brought out the orange in it.

I wonder if it is a message from my subconscious that I must be more religious?

Monday June 20th
8:00 a.m.

The Portly One (Vati) yelled up, "Georgia, up NOW! You've got five minutes to get your bum down here."

Oh, he is so crude. And how dare he take my bum's name in vain?

My delightful little sister unexpectedly burst into my room to collect Sandra. She was wearing a see-through plastic Pacamac and some tiny tiny pants that she must have had when she was a baby. Or, more likely, she has nicked them from a poor unfortunate child at playschool. I must tell Mutti to remind the mothers not to leave their toddlers unattended when Libby's around. She came over, quite slowly because the tiny pants were making her walk with small steps, got into bed with me and grabbed Our Lord and started to cuddle him.

I said, "I'm getting up for school now, Bibbs."

She said, "Snuggle buggle."

We had a bit of a cuddle and I kissed the top of her head. Is it normal to be able to snack on Rice Krispies from your little sister's head?

Mutti came bustling in wearing a costume designed for a

teenage prostitute. "Georgia, GET UP! It's ten past eight. You'll be late."

I said, "Late for what? Six hours of misery at Stalag 14 being tortured by the Hitler Youth, followed by twelve hours of extreme boredom and starvation at home?"

She didn't even listen. She said, "Don't be so silly. You are such a drama queen."

Is everyone's life like this?

Cleaning my tushy pegs
Ten minutes later

I wish it was Friday and I could just get it all over with. Masimo comes round and says, "I am sorry, Georgia, I cannot be your one and only one. How do you say in English language? Ah, yes... so long, loser. Loser, loser, double loser, snap snap get the picture?"

Then I could just go back to being ordinarily bored and depressed.

One minute later

I grabbed a piece of toast from the kitchen to ward off death. Angus was happily chewing on something in his basket. He is better fed than me.

On the way out of the front door I heard Mum screeching like a banshee. "Bob, Bob, that horrible furry thing is eating my tights. Stop him, stop him!!! Trap him with that chair!"

Then I heard some crashing and Dad shouting and cursing. Mum hadn't finished: "Of course you haven't broken your leg, Bob. Anyway, never mind about that, get him... Oh bugger, now he's in the laundry room. Oh dear God, he's doing a poo in the ironing. That is it! They are going, they are going!!!"

8:40 a.m.

Jas was on her wall with Tom when I puffed up the hill. They were looking at something in a brown paper parcel. Jas was talking in a really silly girly voice that she uses when Hunky is around. I swear to God she will be developing a lisp soon. Pathetic. She went, "Oooooooohhh, Hunky, that is soooooo interesting. Look at this, Georgia." And she held out the brown paper bag.

There was a newt in the bag. How beyond the Valley of the Really Quite Mad and entering the World of the

Certifiably Bonkers is that?

Jas said, "It's got very unusual markings. I'm taking it into Biology to show Miss Baldwin."

I said, "Yeah, good idea. Crawler."

But she didn't even notice that I'd called her a teacher's botty-kisser because she was so busy being an idiot around her boyfriend.

Tom left us at the corner to go off to college. As he kissed her on her cheek, Jas was fiddling with her fringe so much that I thought she'd had sudden onset of rampant disco inferno dancing. At last they parted. But only after she had blown kisses at him and then he had to pretend to catch them and blow them back for about two trillion years.

She was completely lost in Jasland. "Oh, it is so so so so nice to have him back."

I said, "Is it nice to have him back then?"

But she didn't get it. She just started again. "Oh yes, it is so so so so nice to have him back. I could never not have a boyfriend; it would be so sad. Imagine not having a boyfriend. Oh, actually, I suppose you can imagine not having a boyfriend."

What a cow she can be. I didn't hit her because I think

violence is wrong, and also she was walking too quickly for me to kick. I just said, "You are a very caring person, Jas. It's almost uncanny how empathetic you are."

"I know – do you know what? Sometimes it's like I can actually read Tom's thoughts."

"Really, you mean when he's looking at you and not saying anything, and yet you know what he is thinking?"

"Yeah, like that."

"Yes, I could read his thoughts today too when he was looking at you."

"Really?"

"Yes, it was quite clear he was thinking, *Hey, I've accidentally got a prat for a girlfriend.*"

Hobbling into Stalag 14

I'm not speaking to Jas. She is vair violent. I may have to go to a support group for victims of friends' violence. UNPAL (United Kingdom's Network for Protection Against Loonies).

Assembly

I am at the far end of the Ace Gang lineup next to Rosie. Not in my usual position next to Mad Dog Jas. She has given Ellen, Jools, Mabs and Ro Ro Midget Gems from her secret stash, but I don't care because I am giving her my cold shoulders. She's only got a boyfriend in the first place because of my excellent stalking skills. If it wasn't for me, she would still be Mrs Sad on the shelf of life.

one minute later
Like me.

Oh God.

Even Rosie doing her shoulder disco dancing during "Jerusalem" failed to work its usual magic. Although when she sang, "And was Jerusalem builded here amongst these dark satanic pants", I did snap and join in with the laughing attack the Ace Gang had. We had to be shuussshed by the Hitler Youth.

Slim, our beloved elephantine headmistress, was in full jelloid mode. She was wearing an unusually attractive jumper in canary yellow. It must have taken at least ten sheep to make it. When she loses her rag she trembles all over. But each bit trembles independently. Chins, jowls, basoomas. If there was such a thing as jelly wrestling, she would be top at it.

One minute later

Oh, drone on. Yawn yawn. What was she talking about?

"...No loitering without intent in the loos... In my day you were lucky to get a shoe to live in... Only nineteen more days to go till our production of *Macbeth* – I hope you're all telling your parents about it..." Blah blah blah. As if.

Then through the dark mists of boredom like a hearing-eye dog I heard my name mentioned. As I drifted back into consciousness I heard her say, "Georgia Nicolson and Rosie Mees to see me in my office immediately after assembly."

Oh dear God, what fresh hell?

I looked at Rosie and she looked back. I shrugged my shoulders, she shrugged back. I looked at the Ace Gang and shrugged my shoulders and they shrugged back. (The Ace Gang, I mean, not my shoulders. I don't mean my shoulders have a shrugging life of their own.)

What have we done?

As we were walking out in a Winter Wonderland of shrugging, Hawkeye appeared from nowhere like the Bride of Dracula and barked out, "Stop that shrugging!"

I said to Rosie, "Now shrugging is a capital offence, apparently. Don't accidentally shake your head, for God's sake."

In the waiting room of fear there are Rosie and I and a couple of scaredy first formers playing with their pigtails. Oo-er. Ro Ro said, "Do you remember when the Bummer twins had a pigtail-cutting extravaganza?"

Ah, the Bummers. Jackie and Alison. They had taken bullying to new heights before they were expelled for shoplifting. There was for instance their famous using of first formers as armchairs. And in a particularly inspired moment they had actually superglued one of the little titches to a bench. In their pigtail campaign they used to snip off bits of first formers' pigtails as they passed by and then hang them on their havvies like scalps.

Rosie said, "I wonder what has happened to the Bummers?"

I said, "Prison with a bit of luck."

Two minutes later

Slim had the scaredy little ones in first. They came out about five minutes later all red and crying and hiccupping. I gave one of them a snot rag and asked, "What did you do?"

46

Ginger titch said, "We... we... drew a picture of a vole with a... a... bra on... on the blackboard in... in... blodge."

I said, "Well done, girls, keep up the good work; we are relying on you."

Rosie slapped them both on their backs, a bit hard actually. I thought their lungs might shoot out. She said, "Goodus workus, smallus idiotus." And they went off looking really pleased.

I said, "I like to think they look up to us as examples of womanhood."

And Rosie said, "Yes, but what you have to keep in mind is that you are bonkers."

Then we heard our beloved leader shout out, "Come."

Here we go. A duffing up for something that we quite clearly have not done. Whatever it is.

Slim was scribbling away at her desk. The chair she must have been sitting on (unless she was levitating) was completely hidden from view by her jelloidness. I wonder if she has a specially reinforced chair? There is probably a specialist circus furniture shop where she gets her requirements. Imagine the size of her bath! Oh nooooo, now I've got a nuddy-pants Slim in my head!

Slim finally looked up.

What had we done?

"I am returning these to you."

Wow, this was a turn up for the book! And she handed me a bag. It was the bison horns!!! The return of the bison horns! Yesss! The horns brought back especially from Hamburger-a-gogo land for the Ace Gang. I fondled the horns and thought back to when I had first worn them riding a bucking-bronco bar stool in Gaylords while *Rawhide* played. Let no one say that the Hamburgese have given us no culture besides Elvis. In fact, as I have said many times to those who will listen (i.e., no one), we have a lot to thank our tiny American chums for – mostly things beginning with "h": hamburgers, hillbillies, howdy doody, er... horns and so on.

Slim was still rambling on. "Now I like a joke as much as the next person, but there is a time and a place, and wearing bison horns during German is not the place. Ironically, you two are quite bright girls, but you waste your talents on silliness. You won't get a job as a silly person, you know."

I didn't say "Miss Wilson has" because, as Slim says, there is a time and a place for everything and time waits for nomads, etc.

I was pleased to have the horns back and it made me think quite kindly about Slim. She isn't such a bad old huge elephantine thing, really. When we got to her door to go, I did think about pretending to be a hilarious alien like in *Doctor Who* and saying, "I offer you my mandible in peace." But then I thought, er, no.

German

Herr Kamyer seems to have accidentally come to work dressed as a twit. His trousers are so short they are bordering on the Bermuda shorts area of legwear. And there is never an excuse for wearing a sleeveless jerkin with diamond patterns all over it. Even if you have been brought up on a diet of *spangleferkel*.

I stared at him. He was quite literally a sight for sore eyes. If you looked at him, he gave you sore eyes. He can always be relied on to come up trumps in the twit arena. He blinked back at me. "*Guten morgen*, Georgia and Rosie."

We clicked our heels together and said, "*Jawohl Kommandant*."

I sat next to Rosie in our comfy seats on the back row. In some of our lessons we are not allowed to sit together for some mad reason that escapes me. Something to do with attention deficit disorder. I got out my chuddie and settled down on my arms to have a little zizz. But I could feel mad beadies looking at me. I opened my eyes. It was Jas. Just looking at me. Look all you want, Miss Looking at Me Person. She soooo wanted to know why we had been to Duffing Up Headquarters and come back looking so pleased. But she will be the last to know anything about me now.

Fifteen minutes later

It is impossible to get a decent sleep in German – you just drift off and the shouting begins. It's all *Achtung!* or *Schnell!* and *Raus raus!* and more *Spangleferkel!* Cor blimey. I was awake now, so I might as well do something. I got the horns out. I nudged Rosie awake and said, "Look at my lap."

She said, "As I've said before, Georgia, you are an attractive girl and everything but I'm just not interested."

I said, "No, really look. Take a good look. Drink in the sight. The bison horns are back!" I made up a little dance with the horns on either hand.

Rosie said, "Sound out the bells of England – the fun days are back!"

Break

Yes indeed, even though I am on the rack of luuurve I have the bison horns to comfort me. As we ambled off to Ace Gang Headquarters behind the fives court I said, "Do you know I can feel it in my waters, the bison horns are a symbol of hope. The fact that Slim gave them back is a sign from Baby Jesus, it is the dawn of a new era."

Ellen said, "What, er, do you... er, do you mean that people will be more spiritual and get back to nature and looking after the earth and..."

Is she mad? I said, "No, what it means is that Masimo will be mine, mine all miney mine mine."

I said it to the gang, apart from Jas, who I was *ignorez-vous*ing like billio. She was doing reverse *ignorez-vous*ing by pretending to be interested in what Ellen was saying. I said to the others, "In some ways I am looking forward to the autumn term because of course it means the return of the beret. Imagine the scene: a cold morning at Stalag 14, the grey day stretches ahead filled with lesbian perverts and sadistic 'teachers'; but then up the hill, past the Foxwood lads setting fire to their farts and generally being prats, comes a sight to lift the spirits. Could it be? Is it true?

Silhouetted against the sky is an awesome sight. It's the return of the Ace Gang in winter uniform. Berets proudly worn with bison-horn attachments. Yesssss!"

The gang broke into spontaneous Klingon saluting. Maybe everything is going to be all right.

Two minutes later

When we got to our headquarters, Rosie donned her horns. She strolled up and down just enjoying the magnificence of her own horns. Once we all had them on, I said, "Perhaps this is a good time to repeat the Ace Gang manifesto, because some people who shall remain nameless to save them shame – and that means you, Jas – seem to forget about the Ace Gang when boys turn up."

Jas didn't say anything, she just straightened her horns and smoothed down her fringe. In case she was going to have a violent spaz like this morning, I went behind Rosie because my ankle still hurt.

Rosie said, "Yes, one for all and all for one and one for the road and so on."

Jas was still fiddling about with her fringe, so Rosie put her arms round me and Jas and said, "Let bygones be bygones, shake hands and let the rule of Horn reign."

Mabs, Jools and Ellen were all looking at us. Mabs said, "One for all and one for the road and all for one."

I put my hand out first to Jas, which is vair vair nice of me seeing as it was me who was kicked. But that is me all over. Always the first to offer the hand of friendiness.

After a little minute Jas held out her hand. Rosie raised her eyebrows, and the Ace Gang started doing wise(ish) nodding. Rosie said, "Now hug."

Jas gave me a little hug, and I sort of hugged her back. There was a bit of nunga-nunga contact so I leaped back quickly and said, "Er... group hug, group hug."

This culminated in a group hug that nearly made my eyes pop out. Jools was so hyped up, she yelled, "One for all and all for one and all in a one for... anyway, hip hip hooray for Merrie England and the Ace Gang!!!"

We finished up with a sailor's hornpipe (which I have to say was a spontaneous idea of mine, because England is after all a seafaring nation and renowned for its hornpipes).

Then Wet Lindsay and Astonishingly Dim Monica came round the corner, wearing their prefect badges. How uncool is that? Vair vair uncool is the answer. They are always following us about – haven't they got lives? Lindsay has done something alarming to her head. Her hair has somehow grown a foot over the weekend. (I mean twelve inches; I don't mean that there was a foot coming out of her head, although there might as well be.) She's had extensions. What a mistake. They are spectacularly chav and naff. She said, "Aaaah, are you little girls practising games for one of your pyjama parties? Will there be lemonade and biscuits?"

How could Masimo even think of snogging her? Erlack a pongoes. I drew myself up with great dignitosity and adjusted my horns, which had slightly fallen over one eye in the excitement of the hornpipe. "Your hair is looking unusually, er, unusual, Lindsay, if you don't mind me saying?"

"I mind you saying anything. In fact I mind you breathing."

The bell rang then for end of break. And she went on: "Get back inside, because if one of you is a minute late, it's a bad conduct mark for you all."

Oooooh, fear factor ten. Not. But we all went grumbling and moaning off towards the science block. Lindsay yelled after us. "And take those horns off, you stupid idiots."

I said, "Charming, what a charming charming person she is. In every single way charming."

4:15 p.m.

Walking home with Jas and Ro Ro. Jas has even done linky-upsies with me. She can't stand being unfriends with me, really. Especially as something vair *merde* and *odure* has happened.

Ro Ro said, "I can't believe our horns have been confiscated AGAIN. How crap is life in Stalag 14? Vair vair crap, is the answer. We should write to the newspapers about it. We are almost bound to be drug addicts by the time we are seventeen because of all the trauma."

I said, "We'd only had them back for two hours. It is so so crap. Once again we are hornless."

Jas said, "Not only that but we've got detention for two nights."

I said to her, "Have you thought about going to hospitals and cheering people up, Jas? Because if you have, don't – that's all I'm saying."

Rosie said, "When we started the bison dance in blodge,

♡

I thought Miss Baldwin was busy looking at Jas's newt."

Jas said, "She was. She was very interested in its peculiar markings. Tom said that actually it was the only one of its kind that—"

I said, "Jas, can you shut up now?"

She of course got the immediate hump and said, "It was the stools crashing over that attracted her attention."

Merde.

Jas went on raving on to me, "And even then I think she might have let us off. But you just had to cheek her."

What? What? Why was it my fault? I said that to Mrs Prissypants, "Why does the finger of shame always point towards me?"

Jas went rambling on, "Because when she asked you what you were doing, you said that it was a Viking day of celebration. That was when she snapped."

Booo.

After Jas went home, Rosie and I did a bit of skipping to raise our spirits. I think our skipping days are numbered, though, my nungas are vair heavy. We had to sit down on a bench near the park.

Home

All quiet on the Loon front. I slumped down on the sofa.

Oh God – Tues, Weds, Thurs and all of Friday to go before I know my luuurve fate. Why does he need a week to think about it? Why didn't he just say, "Of course I want to be your one and only. You are a Sex Kitty of the first water."

Dave the Laugh would have said that.

One minute later

I miss seeing Dave the Laugh, actually, but I don't feel I can call him. I still don't know what he meant about me not getting it about me and him. Get what?

I thought he said we were only young once and we must blow our horns.

Does he mean he only wants to blow my horn?

Oo-er.

No he can't mean that.

Can he?

Ten minutes later

When Masimo said he would let me know in a week, I wonder if that's a week boy time or week girl time? If a girl says a week, that's what she means, but a boy's week could mean anything. It's like when I say "s'later" to the Ace Gang, that's what I mean – see you later. But when a boy says "s'later" it could mean "you're dumped".

Twenty minutes later

Oh, this is sooooo boring. I'm going out to the park to practise my pretend confident walking where I have got room to really swing my arms. I'll see if it works and anyone thinks I'm confident.

Park

Here we are. So, shoulders back, swingy arms, walking, walking and swing, swing. Feet directly in front of me in a straight line. Make my hips go from side to side. This is a well known boy-entrancing movement. Swing, swing, hip, hip. Aaah yes, this is working, I am feeling very confident. Hello, tree, I am vair vair confident. Head up.

And that's when I saw Dave the Laugh ambling along with his mates. I hadn't seen him since the "what if we should have really been together" incident. Oh, please let him be normal and not *ignorez-vous* me. He saw me and looked across the road, just looking, not smiling. Oh no. This was awful. He didn't want to be my mate any more. I felt a bit like crying.

But then he shouted across, "*Ciao*, Georgia. *Ho due gatti e un maialino!*"

I said, "What?"

He shouted, "I thought you luuurved the Pizza-a-gogo language. I thought you loved Italian blokes. You know, all that handbags at dawn, 'Ooh, have you seen my lovely trousers?' sort of thing. 'Ooo, don't let the rain spoil my hair.'"

Oh dear, he was going to be mean to me and hold a grudge and so on. He was going to be Dave the Unlaugh. But then he smiled at me. He has ever such a nice smiley smile. I was so relieved. I smiled back, and I didn't even rein in my nostrils, I was so pleased we were friends. He didn't come over or anything, though, he just went walking on with his mates. Then he called back, "Oy, missus, you don't know what I said to you in Pizza-a-gogo-ese, do you?"

I said, "Er, yeah."

And he said, "You don't."

"I might."

"Yeah, you might, but you don't. I said, 'I have two cats and a small pig.'"

♥ 59

"That's a lie."

He said, "Is it, though?"

What is he on about?

Then he tapped his nose. "See you Friday at the *MacUseless* rehearsal. Get your pants ready for action!"

Cheeky cat.

Still, he was sort of friendly, so maybe he still likes me. I hope he still likes me.

Two minutes later

I still don't know what he meant about what if you liked someone and let them go.

Does he really mean me and him?

Is he saying he would like to go out with me as my proper boyfriend?

One minute later

Why would he say he has two cats and a small pig?

Boys are without doubt a complete and utter mystery.

And that is *le* fact.

Without doubtosity.

Walking up my road

Oscar was outside his house. He was doing keepie-uppie, listening to his personal stereo and casually eating a Mars bar at the same time. He said, "All right?" in what he fondly imagines is a cool way.

But he took his eye off the ball and it went over the wall. He pretended he had meant to do it by falling to his knees and going, "Yesssss!" like he had scored a goal.

What is the matter with boys?

8:00 p.m.

How disgusting is this? Mum said Angus has eaten her tights and that if I see them poking out of his bum-oley, I must pull them out!

I said to her, "Mum, are you so short of tights that you will wear some that have been in Angus's bum-oley?"

And she said, "No, I just want to strangle him with them."

She is a vair violent and unreasonable person.

In bed

11:00 p.m.

I am using positive thinking and swinging my arms around a lot as I make up an acceptance speech for when the Luuurve God says he wants to go out with me.

OK, this is my acceptance speech: "Aah, Masimo, what a lovely surprise to see you— Owwww, you furry freak!!!"

That isn't the speech. Gordy just leaped off the wardrobe and used my head as a landing pad so he didn't have to hurt his feet leaping straight on to the floor.

Anyway, on with my acceptance speech: "Aah, Masimo, *che bella sorpresa*! What a nice surprise to see you this..." Hang on, what is Italian for "this evening"? This nightio? That can't be right – he'll think I am talking about my jimjams for some reason. I'll look it up later in my *Italian for Complete Fools* book. Anyway, on with the acceptance speechio: "Oh, you would like me to be your girlfriend? Well, that would be *mucho bello*. Grassy arse."

Short and to the point; I think that is the key.

Tuesday June 21st

7:30 a.m.

Had a dream about Masimo last night, only he wasn't speaking in a nice Pizza-a-gogo land accent; he was saying things like, "That is well good" and "Shut it, my son". And most alarmingly he was in a band called the Blunder Boys. I was at the gig and he came over to me and said, "Get your tracksuit top, you've pulled." And as we rode off on his scooter, he started singing, "The Funky Moped" by Jasper Carrot. I've woken up in a cold sweat. What can it mean?

Wednesday June 22nd

6:00 p.m.

How long can this torture go on? On one hand the days seem very very long, like creeping along snaily days; on the other hand it's only a matter of hours until Friday. How many hours exactly? Well, it's 6:00 p.m. now, so that means plus six tonight and then plus twenty-four for tomorrow, and then... er, well, what time will he phone on Friday? Will he count from the hour he told me he would tell me in a week's time? I would. It was 5:45 p.m. last Friday when he told me, so a week would be 5:45 p.m. this Friday. But you never know with boys. What if he counts it from when he got home? Would that be 6:15 p.m? Or maybe he didn't go straight home; maybe he went to the shops and got a few nibbly things, then bumped into someone, so he didn't actually get home until 8:00 p.m. Oh God.

6:30 p.m.
Phoned Jas in sheer desperadoes.

"Jas, do you think he will phone me or come round?"

"Erm, I dunno."

"Yeah, but what do you think? What would you do if you were going to tell me whether you wanted to go out with me?"

"Er... but I don't want to go out with you. I would just tell you. In fact, I am just telling you now."

"Jas, you are being what is technically known as a fool."

She of course, classically, immediately for no reason, got the megahump. But I was in no mood for her humps. I said, "What does Tom think?"

She said, "Hang on, I'll ask him."

Good grief, are they joined at the hip?

She came back a few mins later and said, "Tom says he

will do a bit of detective work and see if he can find out anything."

I said thanks, but in my heart of hearts I don't know if letting Radio Jas find out things is the best foot forward. Too late now.

8:30 p.m.
Tom is going to the snooker club tonight and the Stiff Dylans are playing in a tournament there. Ohgoddygodgod.

Midnight
Jas says she will tell me anything she finds out tomorrow because Tom is going to call her first thing. How am I supposed to sleep under these conditions?

Thursday June 23rd
Banging on Jas's door
7:50 a.m.
Jas's mum answered the door all washed and dressed normally. And smiling. Crikey. It's so relaxing and normal round here; no wonder Jas has got a boyfriend and is not on the rack of love all the time. She has been brought up

properly, not dragged up by fools like I have.

Jas's mum said, "Would you like a piece of toast, dear, or maybe a boiled egg?"

A boiled egg!! Wow it was like being in a *Famous Five* book – the next thing you knew, Jas's dad would come bounding in with a cheery smile and a newspaper.

One minute later

Jas's dad came bounding in with a cheery smile and a newspaper. What is even more amazing is that although he smiled at me, he didn't say anything. Nothing. How cool is that? He didn't ask me anything or tell me a crap joke, he just went off to read his paper. Like a proper dad. He has probably got a pipe.

One minute later

He HAS got a pipe!!!

And he doesn't even light it. He just sucks on it in a pleasant way and doesn't annoy people with smoke, etc.

Amazing.

Walking along to Stalag 14
8:30 a.m.

Waiting for Jas to tell me about the snooker-hall thing. I'm not going to ask her; I have too much pridenosity. She was doing tuneless humming. Very annoying. Then she started talking about *MacUseless* and her part as Lady Macbeth. Who cares about her? She said, "Have you practised your crying for the bit when Macduff finds out his wife and children have been killed?"

I just looked at her. If she thinks it is *me* that should practise crying, she's wrong; it's *her* – if she carries on rambling about rubbish for a bit longer.

But she is as sensitive as a brick. She just went on, "You know when I do the spot thing, well... do you think it should be 'OUT, damned spot'? Or 'Out, DAMNED spot'? Or 'Out, damned SPOT'?"

Finally I snapped. If she thinks I can talk about spots at a time like this, she is madder than I thought. Which doesn't seem possible. I said, "It's irrelevant how you say spot, Jas."

She got all huffy. "No, I think it carries the whole production."

"I'm not talking about the production. I'm just saying it's

♥ 67

irrelevant how you say spot because you won't be alive for *MacUseless* unless you tell me what happened last night at snooker. What did Tom say?"

She looked a bit shifty and began fiddling with her fringe. I resisted slapping her hand. Then she said, "Do you want a bit of chuddie?"

"No."

"What about a black Midget Gem? They are your fave and—"

"Jas."

"Well, remember, don't shoot the messenger."

"What?"

"I'm just telling you because you asked me to; it's not my fault as such."

Assembly

Apparently Lindsay had turned up at the snooker hall and stayed for about twenty minutes talking to Masimo, and then slimed off. I tried asking Jas if they looked like they were having snoggy talk, but she said that Tom had gone back to playing snooker. Typical of boys. They think about such rubbish. Tom can't even tell me what Lindsay was wearing, but apparently he told Jas every single score of each game he played and how long each game lasted.

Who cares about that?

My life is double *merde*. And a half. And that is a fact.

Break

The Ace Gang did their best to keep my spirits up. But even Rosie tucking her skirt into her knickers and walking into class as if she looked perfectly normal couldn't cheer me up.

And I'm sure Wet Lindsay was deliberately shaking her ludicrous extensions about like a ninny to show me that she had spoken to Masimo. With a bit of luck she will catch them in a locker and her head will come off.

In bed
7:30 p.m.

Under the covers. With the lights out.

Mum bustled in. She said, "What are you doing in bed?"

I said from under the covers, "Oh, you know, the shot put, that sort of thing." What does she think I am doing in bed with the light off?

She immediately got the hump, obviously: "You are so

♡

rude, Georgia. It's not my fault you've got obsessed with some boy. And I'm not your servant, either. You just come in and drop your things anywhere. I'm a person, you know, not just here to tidy up after you and cook and clean."

That perked me up, despite my tragicosity. I sat up and removed my cucumber eye patches. "Cook and clean? Clean?? Cook?? I had a cheese sandwich for my dinner, and that is after double maths. AND I made the sandwich. AND Gordy ate half of it when I was scrabbling in the fridge hoping there might be something green in there to save me from rickets. There was something green in there as it happens, but I don't like MOSS."

Mum shouted, "Oh, here's an idea – why don't YOU clean the fridge sometime? And, anyway, don't I have any right to be myself? You know I've got aerobics on Thursdays. It keeps me in shape."

I said, "Wrong."

She stormed out then in a huff and a tizz and a strop: "You are HORRIBLE!!!"

And she slammed the door. How childish.

7:45 p.m.

I'm not horrible. She's horrible.

8:00 p.m.

What time is it now?

Only eight o'clock. Oh dear God.

9:00 p.m.

I can't sleep. I may even have to do my French homework to take my mind off Masimo and Lindsay. What were they talking about for twenty minutes?

9:10 p.m.

Here we go. Chapter fourteen in my French textbook. Jools and Jim and their fantastic excursion to the Bois de Boulogne. Why are they so excited about going to some woods? It's like reading the froggy version of Jas and Tom. I could write a book called *Jas and Tom and Their Fantastic Excursion to the Bois de Boulogne*.

Clearly no one would buy it because it would be so boring.

Samedi

Jas a dit avec sa bouche stupide, "Ooooohhh, c'est magnifique, c'est la bonne newt!!!"

Tom a dit, "Oh lalalala."

Les idiots chantent, "Non, je ne regrette rien!!!!"

And so on. What larks!!! I wonder what happens next? I can't wait! Perhaps they find some *escargots* and... zzzzzzzzzzzzzzzz.

on the brink of madnosity

Friday June 24th

Dawn

Birds singing, clouds cludding, heart thudding. What if he comes to meet me after Stalag 14? What if he just decides spontaneously to come to school and pick me up? That's what boys do. They don't think about the preparation that has to be done – make-up and mood planning and so on.

Oh Blimey O'Reilly's trousers.

Also, if he was thinking the age gap was a bad thing, the last thing he needs to see is me in my stupid school shirt and tie. I must take a change of clothes just in case. I'll have to dash off to the tarts' wardrobe after the *MacUseless* rehearsal.

one minute later

But what if he doesn't know about the *MacUseless* rehearsal and comes at the normal time they open the prison gates?

Even if I keep things to the minimum – lip gloss, foundation, mascara – it is still going to take me ten minutes, and the changing as well. Oh, this is so stressful. Why do we have to go to school? I've been going for the last ten years and where has it got me? Still at school, that's where it has got me.

7:40 a.m.

Packing my rucky. I've put in my clothes and essential make-up. So clearly there is no room for my books and homework. *C'est la vie.* Anyway, I am only going to school in the first place to fill in time and to stop my mutti and vati going to jail. I don't know why I bother, though. Mum is still *ignorez*ing me. She is so vair vair immature.

8:10 a.m.

Mum didn't even say good morning or look at me when I rustled around in the kitchen. She is still having the hump and strop because of what I said about her shape. You know, not having one. Maybe that was going just that tiny bit too far.

8:15 a.m.
Maybe not, though. When Mum bent over to hand Libby a spoon for her eggy and soldiers, she knocked over a cup of tea with her nunga-nungas.

8:20 a.m.
I said, "S'laters" as I went, but Mrs Giant Basoomas didn't say anything.

My lovely sister didn't ignore me though, unfortunately. She snogged me and said, "Here is your runch, Ginger, yum." And gave me a bit of soldier with egg on it. It is not as such unchewed.

8:30 a.m
Jas is being "cool". It is vair vair vair annoying and driving me to the brink of madnosity.

I wanted to know what she thought the Luuurve God would decide. She knows this is the big decision day. She is trying to be philosophical about my situation, like she is some beardy monk or something. She said, "*Que sera, sera,*

♥

whatever will be, will be, the future's not ours to see, *que sera, sera*."

I said, "Don't say *que sera* again, Jas, unless you want a duffing incident."

She just raised her eyebrows, but I know that she is deliberately saying *que sera* in her brain.

Assembly

We shuffled into the main hall past Droopy Drawers Lindsay and her astonishingly dim mate Monica. No sign of Hawkeye, seeing-eye dog and *Oberführer*. Oh dear, I hope she hasn't been accidentally kidnapped by squids.

Slim is dressed entirely in brown today, which makes her look like a giant onion bhaji. As usual, she had something depressing to say: "Settle, girls." We resisted doing our cooing-like-pigeons thing because she was on a rampage extraordinaribus. She said, "It has come to my attention that some of you girls are rolling your school skirts over at the waistband to make them shorter. Madame Slack said that she saw a group of girls this morning, and at first from a distance she thought they had forgotten to put their skirts on at all. This is a ridiculous practice and gives the school a bad name. It will cease forthwith."

Oh, ramble on, why don't you? Has she really not got anything else to think about? What is so vair vair wrong with showing a bit of knee to cheer up the nation?

Slim had finished with knees and was now on to something even more boring. "And now to fire precautions – a most important and serious subject. Mr Attwood has something to say to you."

I said to Ro Ro, "Let's hope it's 'goodbye'."

Ro Ro said, "I thought he was supposed to be retiring. Why is he still alive? Why hasn't he gone to that big caretakers' home in the sky?"

Elvis shuffled his way up on to the stage and adjusted his glasses. "Thank you, Headmistress. I am sorry to say that during last week's play rehearsal in the main hall, various incidents involved the unlawful use of fire extinguishers. They have been used in what some idiots like to call 'foam fights'. I was caught in one of these so-called 'foam fights' and have only just recovered proper hearing in my left ear. But even more serious is the fact that I came across one of my fire blankets being put over the vaulting horse in the gym by a Foxwood lad. When I asked the culprit why he had removed an important part of firefighting equipment, he said (and Elvis looked at his sad snitching diary), 'I thought the horse might be chilly, because even though it's June the nights can turn quite nippy noodles.'"

The Ace Gang had a laughing spaz, but we had to change it into coughing in case of a bad-conduct-mark-all-round fandango. I had forgotten about the gym horse and Dave the Laugh incident. I might have known Elvis would have snitched.

Elvis was still going on. "Would that lad have found it funny if he had caught fire and the blanket I would have normally used to extinguish him was missing? Do any of you see the joke now?"

I half put my hand up, but Madame Slack was on substitute glaring duty in Hawkeye's absence, so I had to turn it into scratchy ear.

Happy happy days! Apparently Hawkeye is off today, brushing up her girl hating skills at some convention (the cruelty convention probably). She'll come back with a whip and an Alsation next week. But on the plus side, I can put as much make-up on as I like this aftie! We only have Miss Wilson and Herr Kamyer. Hooorah!!!

Behind the fives court
Break time

I said to the Ace Gang, "I am sooooooo nervous. I feel an f.t. coming on, quickly followed by a nervy b. If I smoked, you wouldn't be able to see my head for smoke. I would be smoking ten at a time. And I would have a pipe as well. Say something to calm me down."

Ellen said, "What time... what time will he call... I mean, did he say he would call or did he say see you later... because if he did, I mean if he did the s'later thing, well, that would mean... well, I don't know what that would mean."

I said, "Thanks very much for that, Ellen."

Jools said, "What exactly is the point of boys?"

Mabs said, "Pardon?"

Jools said, "I mean really, what is the point of having them around?"

Rosie said, "Snogging."

Jools said, "Yeah, fair point, but besides that? I mean, take Rollo. I like him and everything, but he turns up and we go to the pictures and snog. Or we go for a walk and we snog. Or we just snog. Which is nice. But the fact is, mostly I don't know what on earth he is going on about. He says

♥ 79

stuff like, 'I've got the entire collection of first-edition *Beano* comics.' What am I supposed to think about that?"

We did supportive shrugging.

Rosie said, "I think your mistake is thinking you should talk to him. It's so much more soothing to have a foreign boyfriend who is also mad."

Jas got up on to her high horsey knickers and said, "Well, I think you are wrong, Rosie. Tom and I do all sorts of things together. We go beyond just snogging."

I went, "Ooooo-er."

But she was off into Jasland. "I mean, I think the important thing is to choose someone that you have things in common with."

Oh, please don't let her go on about molluscs.

Rosie was stuffing a Jammy Dodger into her gob, but she still managed to drop *le* bombshell: "Oh yes, I so agree. That is why Sven and I are going to get married."

What?

We all looked at her.

She looked back.

I said, "No, you're not."

Rosie opened her mouth and showed me her half-eaten

Jammy Dodger. Good grief. Has the strain of going out with Sven finally driven her to unusual levels of bonkerosity?

Two minutes later

Even though I tried to make Rosie admit she was joshing, she insists she is a bride to be. I said, "Oh yes, and when did you become a bride to be? Was it a minute ago, when you got bored with Jas talking about her and Hunky?"

Rosie said, "You have a very suspicious mind, Georgia. Sven proposed to me many weeks ago."

I said, "How did you know what he was asking you? Normally no one can understand a word he says."

Rosie said, "His eyes spoke for him."

"Now he's got talking eyes?"

She was talking absolute poppycock and balderdash and woopsie.

However, Ellen had got really carried away with the excitement of Rosie's forthcoming imaginary wedding. She said, "Oh, I love weddings. Can I be a bridesmaid?"

Rosie said, "Yep, you can all be bridesmaids. I am thinking of asking Herr Kamyer to be matron of honour. He's got the legs for it."

As the bell rang I said to the blushing bride to be, "What do your parents think about it? Are they, you know, over the moon that you are getting married at fifteen and a half to a madman?"

She said, "Oh yes."

Maths

Even though I know she is talking absolute pants, Rosie has managed to take my mind off my own life. Sometimes for moments at a time I can forget I am on the rack of luuurve.

One minute later

Which reminds me – only four hours to countdown. I'd better start applying my base coat of foundation. I'll do base coat, highlights and first coat of mascara in maths, and then I can continue with the second coat and first coat of eye shadow in physics. Miss Wilson won't tell me off. And even if she did try, I would convince her that I was just getting into my character. Because as everyone knows, Scottish lairds used to wear woad and so on.

Five minutes later

It's quite hard putting on mascara when you have to practically lie down on your desk to not be spotted. Honestly, school is soooo annoying. And pointless. Miss Stamp is going on about pi again. Which reminds me, I'm a bit peckish. I wonder if Jazzy Spazzy has any Wotsits secreted about her person.

Rosie has started sending notes:

Dear all,

Sven and I have decided on a Viking wedding in honour of Sven's roots. This will involve a lot of heavy lifting as the bride and bridegroom are traditionally carried around town on a replica longboat. I suggest you all start a regime of fitness. And I am thinking particularly of Ellen. I do not want the festivities spoiled by any suggestion of lardiness.

Yours sincerely,

the Bride to Be

p.s. I will be compiling a wedding gift list shortly.

p.p.s. In the meantime any spare chuddie would be appreciated.

I wrote back:

Dear Bride to Be,

Hopefully we will have the bison horns back in time for the wedding. By the way, when is it?

Yours sincerely,

a friend and well-wisher

Afternoon break

It turns out that the wedding is planned for Rosie's twenty-first birthday.

I said, "Forgive me if I'm right, but that is in more than five years' time."

Rosie said, "Yes, but you can't rush a Viking wedding. There are vats to be found."

"Vats?"

"Oh yes, for the mead and so on. Shall I show you a Viking version of 'Let's go down the disco' that we could do at the reception?"

I said, "No, my base coat might run."

"Come on, you'll like it A LOT!"

She made us all trudge across to the fives court and showed us the new Viking disco inferno dance. Before I knew it, we were all doing it. We sang along to "Jingle bells, jingle bells" because although Rosie is allegedly the world expert on Viking-a-gogo land, she doesn't know any Viking songs.

I said, "What's wrong with 'Edelweiss' from *The Sound of Pants* musical?"

But as usual Mrs Prissy Knickers Jas said, "That is an Austrian song. About Austria. Which is not Svenland."

Here we go. She is absolutely obsessed with countries and where they are.

I said, "Look, Jas, it's a practice Viking dance, and number one, Rosie isn't getting married for five years and probably not even then, and number two, we don't know where Sven comes from anyway. And number three, you are annoying me and forgetting to remember that I am on the rack of luuurve."

That made her shut up. She should think of others more than herself.

I do.

I don't know why, though, because it is really boring and pointless.

Ten minutes later

We have perfected the Viking disco inferno dance. Even though I say it myself, it is a triumph. And once the horns are returned, the whole thing will have *je ne sais quoi* and harummph and possibly Good Lordnosity.

Just before we went in for an afternoon of sheer unadulterated *merde* (physics), Rosie yelled, "OK. One last time, let's hit it, lads! Jingle bells, jingle bells, jingle all the way. Oh, what fun it is to ride on a one-horse open sleigh-ay!!!"

And then all together we did the dance. Stamp, stamp to the left, left leg kick, kick. Arm up, stab, stab to the left (that's the pillaging bit). Then stamp, stamp to the right, right leg kick, kick. Arm up, stab, stab to the right. Quick twirl round with both hands raised to Thor (whatever). Then raise your (pretend) drinking horn to the left, drinking horn to the right, raise your horn to the sky, all over body shake, huddly duddly and fall to knees with a triumphant shout of "HORRRRNNNNN!!!!"

Yesss!

MacUseless rehearsals
4:10 p.m.
I have completed my make-up pre-make-up preparations. On the way down to the hall I saw Wet Lindsay laying into the first formers who had done the picture of a vole with a bra on. She had them pinned up against the wall. They were looking really scared. They had probably seen her knees. Wet Lindsay was saying to the titches, "Why were you outside the school gates at lunchtime? Well?"

They didn't say anything. They were just staring at her and blinking like she was a sort of octopus who had just leaped out and was asking them questions. It is an easy mistake to make with her no forehead and hair extensions. I wonder if Masimo has seen her head lately? Oh yes, he must have, I have just remembered the snooker fiasco.

Merde. And also how pathetic is she, trailing around after Masimo? Anyway, Octopus Head was still raving on: "Well, I'm waiting! What were you doing outside the school gates?"

The titch sisters started blubbing even more, and one said, "I... ddddddon't knnnnow."

Lindsay said, "Ah, you don't know. Well, I tell you what I'll do – I'll let you have a long think about it. Until you do know. And while you are thinking, you can clear out the sports cupboard after school on Monday."

One of them said, "But, but I've got... blub blub... violin practice on Mondays."

Wet Lindsay said, "You *did* have violin practice. Clear off."

The two blubsters went blubbing off down the corridor. As I went by Octopussy I gave her my worst look. But I didn't say anything. Then I just let my eyes fix on a place where her forehead should have been if she'd had one. She put her hand up like she thought she had an antenna growing there or something. Hahahahah yesss! Result! The no-forehead staring campaign continues.

She said, "Are you wearing make-up?"

"It's for the play."

As she was about to go into the common room she said, "A bit of advice, lady – you are making yourself look like a ridiculous tart trailing around after Masimo. It makes you look like what you are: a silly cheap pathetic baby. I think you're ridiculous and he thinks you're ridiculous. He's too nice to say, but he told me he feels really sorry for you. Do yourself and all of us a favour and stop making a fool of yourself. He's out of your league."

Even though I hate her a million and a half and know she's a liar, I did feel my face going all red.

Five minutes later

The Ace Gang were in the tarts' wardrobe getting ready for the Foxwood boys' extravaganza. The whole school was on high-hysteria alert. I even saw a couple of first formers with a bit of lippy on. It's insane, really, because it's not like we're shut up in a convent. Some people really have no self-controlnosity when it comes to boys. I couldn't get near the mirror to check my final make-up, but I like to think I achieved a natural look. Unlike Ellen. Her lip gloss was so thick, she looked like she had plunged her gob into a pot of treacle. Even Jas was using eyelash curlers. Why? Tom wasn't even in *MacUseless*. I said, "Why are you curling your eyelashes when your so-called beloved is not even going to be here?"

She spluttered on about Lady Macbeth, saying that the curly eyelashes were all part of the historical detail, that she would be wearing authentic drawstring pants under her dress, and so on, rambling on. I wish I had never mentioned it.

I told the gang what Lindsay had said.

Jools said, "What a prize bitch."

And Ro Ro said, "Octopussy talks WUBBISH!!"

Mabs said, "Let's kill her. No one would notice."

It's nice that they care and offer sensible advice, but all the same I am still, as Elvis (he dared to rock) Presley said, "all shook up, ah huh."

I said to Jas as we trolled off to the main hall, "She practically said I was stalking Masimo. How could she say that?"

Jas said, "Well, she's got a point. It's just that she doesn't know she has."

"What are you rambling on about now?"

"Well, you tried to find him in Hamburger-a-gogo land, didn't you?"

90

"Well, yeah, but—"

"You remember, when you rang everyone in New York New York called Scarlotti—"

"Well, yeah—"

"And you ended up ordering a Chinese takeaway – from New York. And we were in Memphis."

Oh God, bang on about history, why don't you?

I said, "Jas, that was before I got maturiosity."

Jas laughed.

Which makes her look stupid.

Five minutes later

What if Masimo is at the gates? I will just sneak out in a casualosity at all times way to see if he's there.

Two minutes later

I walked across the side of the playground towards the school gates. No sign of the Luuurve God. Just in case he was hidden from view I did my hip hip, flick flick thing. As I got to the gate Mr Attwood leaped out from the herbaceous border in full madman outfit – overalls and a cap and his fire extinguisher. What is the matter with him?

He said, "What are you doing out here, young lady? You should be in the main hall. If I am not informed of where all personnel are, there might be casualties unaccounted for in the event of major conflagration."

Has the human race come to this?

Back in the tarts' wardrobe for a final make-up check
Ten minutes later

God, I can hardly move my eyes, I've got so much mascara on. I'm so on the edge of having a complete tiz and to do. And on top of everything else I feel a bit nervy and excited about seeing Dave the Laugh.

As we approached the main hall doors I said, "Shall we do a quick burst of the Viking disco inferno backstage to let Dave and his mates know that the *MacUseless* party has begun?"

Jas said, "I don't think Dave the Laugh will want to see anything you have to show him, if you know what I mean."

I glared at her in a meaningful way, but she didn't know what I meant. However, as she had said something about Dave the Laugh, Ellen went off in a dithercab. "Did you say, er, Dave the, er, Laugh wouldn't want to see anything that...

to see anything that Georgia shows him... I mean, what does that mean?"

Fortunately at that moment we entered the hall and her ditherosity was drowned out by the lads cheering and yelling, "Nunga-nungas!!!"

Dave the Laugh was at the front of the mob of lads, pretending to keep them back and saying to us, "Move along, ladeeez, there is nothing to see here. Nothing to see." Like a policeman at a road accident.

6:00 p.m.
After the usual hour and a half of chaos that Miss Wilson calls "rehearsal", we were set loose from Stalag 14. I nipped off to the tarts' wardrobe to roll my skirt up and put my black lacy top on. The Ace Gang were still in *MacUseless* mood. Rosie was doing her "eye of newt" bit but improvising by adding "yum yum". She will probably do it on performance night and then we will all be executed.

But actually that would be a blessing in disguise. I am on the rack of love and feel like going to the piddly-diddly department every five seconds. What if he is there? What should I do? Should I display glacial glaciosity or have just a hint of Eastern promise lurking across my face? I made the Ace Gang walk in front of me so I could reveal myself to him at my best angle when I saw him.

As we walked across the playground I could see that Masimo wasn't waiting outside the school gates to meet me. I felt quite relieved in a way. I don't know why. At least I didn't have to put up with all the ogling oglers looking at me making a prat of myself in front of him. Or fainting, which I probably would have done. Or having a sudden poo-parlour-division episode.

Still, he did say he would let me know in a week, and the week didn't start at the school gates, did it? It started at my house. So I needn't worry until I get to my house.

Two minutes later
I wonder if Masimo would think walking home as a gang was a hoot and a half, or if he would think it was a bit childish? But we don't *always* limp and pretend to be the Hunchbacks of Notre Dame. We only do it when it's appropriate. You know, on boring bits of walking or in lessons. I can be as full of maturiosity as the next person. Ish.

Ten minutes later

Dave and his gang leaped out from behind some bushes and nearly gave us a heart attack. Ellen's head was so red I thought it would explode. I felt funny, sort of pleased that he was with us. Even though it had literally been about ten minutes since I last saw him.

Two minutes later

Dave was doing a really bad backwards moon walk, with his bottom sticking out and his collar up. He was shouting at us, "You are my bitches!!!"

Rollo said, "Leave it out, mate, I'm not that kind of bloke."

Dave said, "No, just the bitches are my bitches!!!"

Ellen, who had turned into a walking beetroot because of Dave, said to me, "Er, do you... er, like, is it OK to call us bitches? Isn't it, like, erm... disrespectful to women?"

I said, "Yes, but he's talking to us."

She said, "Oh yeah, right, I see."

But she clearly doesn't. She soooo luuurves Dave that she would probably wear a false beard if he told her to.

Which incidentally, he might.

Also, it's going to be midnight before she gets home, because she lives in the opposite direction.

Dave was still going on doing the moon walking. He said, "OK, ma bitches, WHO'S THE DADDY?"

I said, "We don't say 'daddy' – we think it's naff. We say 'vati'."

Dave said, "OK, cool, WHO'S THE VATI?"

We just looked at him going backwards, so he shouted again, "WHO'S THE VATI?"

And Jas, Rosie, Ellen, Jools, Mabs and me had to say, "You're the vati."

At which point Dave, otherwise known as The Vati, walked backwards into the low wall of the park and fell over it.

Vair *amusant*.

6:15 p.m.
Just me and Dave now. Ambling along. The others have all gone home. Even Ellen realised that she couldn't go on being hypnotised by Dave like a... er... hypnotised beetroot, and then a bus came along going her way. I think she was half-hoping I would say why didn't she come home with me

and my vati would give her a lift home later. But I just couldn't, not with the Masimo fandango.

As she was going, Ellen said to Dave, "See you next week, then."

And Dave said, "Missing you already."

And Ellen reached new heights of beetrootosity. Oh God, I wonder how long it will be before she is on the blower saying, "You know when he said he was like... er... missing me... well, does that mean... he's, like, missing me, or...?"

After she had gone I looked at Dave with raised eyebrows. He raised his eyebrows back. I raised mine even higher and did the nodding knowledgeably thing. He nodded back.

He knows what I mean, though. He knows that Ellen luuurves him. Even if he didn't, he pretty much seems to think that everyone luuurves him. In fact, he's not wrong. All the girls in the play act in a ludicrous way with him, even when he is vair vair rude. I was glad that we were matey mates and that I didn't feel awkward with him any more. Well, not much. I am still avoiding the topic of the Italian Stallion in front of him.

When Jazzy Spazzy got to her house, she unexpectedly

gave me a little hug and said, "I hope it all goes all right. Ring me later." Which was quite touching. But it did imply that there was something to "go all right" about. To cover up any questions Dave might ask me about what the thing "going all right" was and so on, I said, "Did you see how she hugged me for just that little bit too long. She is definitely on the turn. I must be on lezzie alert. She was looking at my tights when I was gallivanting around as Macduff."

Dave said, "Who *wasn't*?"

I said, "Actually, you weren't. You were being hypnotised by Melanie Griffiths' basoomas."

"You have a very suspicious mind, Kittykat. As you know, I am very safety conscious and I was making sure that Melanie did not topple over and injure herself during the juggling scene."

"Safety conscious?"

"Yep."

"You're mad."

"No, you're mad."

"Er, I think you'll find YOU'RE mad."

Then he got hold of me and started tickling me. Oh no, tickly bears!!! The next stage after tickly bears was usually number four on the snogging scale! My lips even started puckering up like Pavlov's dog's lips.

Then he stopped tickling me. He had both his arms on mine, sort of holding them against my sides. His face was very close, and he looked at me. He had very dreamy eyes. They had that soft, pre-snogging look about them. My brain was trying to have a stiff word with me: "Calling all parts, calling all parts, and that means you, lips! Stop that puckering. We are on pucker alert!!! Remember, remember, you're a Womble! Er, I mean remember you are the nearly-girlfriend of a Luuurve God."

Then, just as my lips developed their own brain and thought, *Oh, sod it, give us a snog!* Dave let me go and said, "Bad bad Sex Kitty. Bye bye."

And he went off.

Blimey, I nearly fell on to the ground when he let me go.

What was the matter with me?

6:25 p.m.
I did hip hip, loosey arms and flicky hair all the way up my street just in case Masimo was waiting for me. But he wasn't.

In my bedroom
6:45 p.m.

In the nuddy-pants in front of the full-length mirror. I have put my dressing table in front of the door so that no one can burst in and surprise me in the rudey dudeys.

If I jump up and down, my nunga-nungas practically slap me in the face.

So I must be sure not to leap up and down in front of Masimo.

Now then. Check list:

Whole body a lurker-free zone? Check.

Orang-utan gene plucked to within an inch of its life? Check.

Four layers of natural foundation? Check.

Shading applied to draw the eye away from less good features, i.e., huge conkerositiness? Well, I've done my best.

Hair not looking like bombhead? Yes, sir.

Lippy and lip gloss applied for that hint of sophisticosity beyond my years and a touch of Eastern promise? Turkish delight-flavoured lip gloss. Mmmm tasty.

Over-the-shoulder-boulder-holder and knick-knacks next. Good. All safely harnessed in.

Now then, clothes, hmmm... Tight jeans, but not so tight that I can't get my leg over... his Vespa. Or should I wear my skirt with the fringey bit on? Yes, yes, that's better.

Is it?

7:00 p.m.

I think I'll put the jeans back on. They seem more casual.

7:15 p.m.

Not as full of SexKittynosity, though. I'll put the skirt back on.

7:30 p.m.

What if it's a bit nippy noodles? Jeans, I think.

7:45 p.m.

Skirt back on.

7:55 p.m.

Jeans, now that is it. I am not changing again.

7:58 p.m.
Skirt!

7:59 p.m.
This is absolutely it. The jeans are on and that is it.

8:00 p.m.
He's still not called. The only slight silver lining is that Swiss Family Mad are out again and I have some privacy.

8:05 p.m.
Phone rang. Oh gadzooks!!! I leaped down the stairs. With Angus and Gordy attached to each leg. I thought they had been suspiciously quiet; they must have been lurking outside my door just waiting for me to come out. They clung on all the way down, even though their heads were bumping against each step. Don't they feel pain?

Sadly not. Got to the phone with my cat-legs and did a lot of calmy calm breathing. Ommmmm.

I picked up the phone.

"Georgia?"

"Jas! Why are you calling me now?"

"Because I wanted to know if you were on the phone to Masimo. I didn't know you were going to answer it."

"Why wouldn't I answer the phone if it rang?"

"Because, as I have explained, it wouldn't have rung if you had been on the phone and—"

"Look, Jas, I have to go."

"He hasn't rung, has he? I can tell. You sound really really bad. Are you feeling awful? I would. Have you been blubbing?"

"No, I—"

"It must be awful being dumped. Especially when you had never really, you know, been—"

"Jas."

"What?"

"Shut up."

"I was just being a chum."

"Well, don't."

"Well, I won't."

"Good."

I slammed the phone down so that she couldn't go off in a strop. I had out-stropped her for once. Ha ha and double ha.

8:10 p.m.

Managed to eventually get the kittys off by spraying them with the shower attachment. I had to be careful to just focus the water on to their heads and not get any on my jeans. They hate the idea of being clean and they leaped off, sneezing and shaking like loonies, and charged outside to roll in some fox poo or something.

8:30 p.m.

Perhaps he's got a Stiff Dylans gig.

9:02 p.m.

Or perhaps Wet Lindsay was telling the truth and he does think I am pathetic. And he feels sorry for me. So that's why he's being nice.

9:03 p.m.

Perhaps he's held up because he is telling Wet Lindsay that she looks like an octopus.

I wish.

9:08 p.m.

Perhaps he is seeing her on a date? Oh noooooo.

Still, girdey loins, girdey loins.

9:10 p.m.

I must consult with my boy manual *How to Make Any Twit Fall in Love with You.*

9:20 p.m.

Oh God goddy God, I have done the wrong thing! It says you shouldn't let boys know that you want something because then they feel under pressure. Ohhhh noooo.

9:30 p.m.

It's true, isn't it? The rule with boys is glaciosity at all times. I remember when Dave the Laugh told me I had inadvertently displayed glaciosity to Masimo when I ran off when he asked for my phone number.

Oh, I wish I could phone up the Hornmeister now. I miss him.

Only in a matey way.

He hasn't said anything nice to me lately.

Although he did say "bad Sex Kitty".

9:32 p.m.
He used to say that despite being certifiably insane I was a lovely, funny person. And that is nice. Just what a proper boy mate would say.

9:33 p.m.
But if he is just a boy mate, how come we got to number six?

9:34 p.m.
But my ad-hoc and red-bottomosity days are over. I will never feel Dave the Laugh's nip-libbling technique again. Which is a shame. Shut up shut up, voice of the Horn.

9:35 p.m.
I don't know why I'm bothering giving up the Horn in my head when in fact no one is asking me to be their one and only girlfriend anyway.

I may as well take off my make-up.

9:40 p.m.

No, why should I bother cleansing and toning? What's the point of having toned skin if there's no one there to say, "Blimey, your skin is toned. Will you be mine?"

Downstairs
9:45 p.m.

I looked out of the front-room window at the dark street. I may as well go to bed. For ever. I looked up at the dark sky. Surely there is some beardy bloke up there somewhere who cares about me? Maybe I should go to church more. My last visit was not what you would call an all-round success – vis-à-vis the accidental pensioner inferno. Which I have to say was a lot of fuss about nothing. The elderly can be vair hysterical. My votive candle merely set fire to the pensioner's headscarf. She shouldn't have worn acrylic material as it clearly is a fire hazard. Even before that, I was having an unlaugh. In his sermon Call-me-Arnold the vicar said, "We all come into the world alone and go out of it alone." I don't know why he bothers going to church just to depress people.

9:46 p.m.

For once he is right, though. I am on my owney. All aloney.

9:48 p.m.

Now I really really am depressed. I am just looking out on to the dark void of life. The long, dark street of life, reaching into the distance of nothingosity.

Then I almost had a nervy spaz because Angus and Gordy suddenly appeared on the windowsill. They were doing pathetic meowing, looking straight into my eyes through the window. Well, Angus was. They were opening their mouths and really wailing.

It was a sign. They had sensed my pain and been drawn towards the front-room window of agony to give me comfort. They were wailing along with my inward wailing.

Except the funny thing was, I couldn't hear anything. I opened the window. And they went on doing the pathetic meowing and looking straight into my eyes. And I realised why I hadn't been able to hear them. They couldn't even be bothered making a noise. They were just doing pretendy silent wailing.

Well, they can stay outside. Why should I be nice to

them? No one is nice to me. Anyway, they just use me for kitty snacks and molesting, and then they go off to play without a second's thought.

I hope it snows.

Four minutes later

That would be quite unusual in midsummer, but it would fit in with my mood.

And serve the furry freak twins right.

In my bedroom
10:00 p.m.

Oh marvellous, the Mads are back. I can hear them singing, "We're all off to Dublin in the green, in the green" in crap Irish accents. I must pretend I'm asleep.

I leaped into bed fully clothed and turned the light off.

I snuggled down in the bed and my feet touched something furry. Which started to purr. The kittykats! How had they snuck into my bed? The tiny top window in my bedroom is open, but how would they get up there? They probably have cat abseiling equipment stashed among Dad's fishing rods in the shed. Too late to drag them out because I could hear an awful noise coming up the stairs. Please, please let it not be Vati coming in to sing Irish songs to me and do sad dancing with his trousers rolled up.

It was Mutti, because I heard her call to Dad, "Bob, make a cup of tea. I'll put Bibbs to bed and just look in at Georgia."

Then I realised what the awful noise was. It was my darling little sister snoring like a stuck pig. The snoring got quieter as Mum went into Libb's bedroom, and I heard her shut the door. Perhaps she would just go away. But no. My door opened and Mum came over to my bed. I could sort of sense her presence with my eyes tight shut. She whispered, "Gee, are you awake?"

I did a pretendy snore. And that's when I felt the kittykats stir. Something wet and rough touched my feet. Oh God, it was their tongues. They were licking me with their horrible cat tongues! Urgh urgh. It was soo disgusting, I couldn't stand it. But I must keep still, I must.

It was like in Latin when we learned about Sparta. Two boys from Sparta went out to steal chickens, and they saw the farmer coming so they put the chickens down the front of their trousers (or whatever Sparta people wore). The farmer said, "Oy, you two lads-us, have-us you seen-us any of my chickens-us?" (That's just a rough Latin translation.)

Anyway, the two boys said, "Your chickens-us? Not us, mate-us."

And the farmer said, "Me think-us you have us..."

And all the time the chickens were pecking and scratching the boys' trouser-snake addenda. Eventually the farmer went off and the boys staggered home, handed over the chickens to their mum and then died of their wounds. And the whole of Sparta honoured them because they hadn't cracked under pressure. As I have said many many times, Latin is crap.

Where was I? Oh yes, anyway, that's what it was like for me. I was being submitted to tongue torture. And I couldn't cry out or anything. Mum touched my hair. As she did, the tongues reached the back of my knees. Oh dear God, if they went beyond the knees, I don't think I could stand it.

10:10 p.m.
At last Mum packed it in and left the room. I turned the light on and ripped back the covers to expose the furry leg-munchers. I said, "Get out of my bed, NOW!!"

They were blinking in the light. Angus put one big paw on my leg and let his claws come out. He was looking at me and I was looking at him with my sternest look. I know very well that he understands me. I am, after all, his mistress. I am his huge baldy mistress and he knows it is his duty to do what I say. Otherwise its goodbye kittykat snacks. He looked and looked and then he let the tip of his tongue pop out of his mouth. He was doing the tongue-lolling idiot-cat thing! Gordy was looking at me with one of his eyes, and then he just nodded off and keeled over.

What is the point?

Angus settled down and nodded off as well. I didn't have the energy to do anything about them, so I pulled the covers up over us all again. I felt like weeping. And I did. Tears started welling up in my eyes. How could this happen to me? I'm not a really bad person. OK, I was a bit snappy with Jas, but that was understandable. I can't bear to go to school again. Lindsay will know what's happened and she will make my life a misery.

I am sooo miserable and lonely.

Two minutes later

The cats started doing violent sneezing under the covers and then started wiggling their way up the bed.

Two minutes later

I have Gordy's head on one side of me and Angus's on the other. I believe they sense my pain.

Five minutes later

Angus put his tongue in my ear!!! How disgusting is that? I might not have a boyfriend, but I have got to number six on the snogging scale with my cat.

Saturday June 25th
8:30 a.m.

Woke up and thought I had gone blind. Actually it was because I hadn't taken my mascara off and my eyes had stuck together.

I trailed down to the loo. No one was up, of course. I could hear snoring from practically every room.

In the bathroom

I looked in the mirror. My hair was completely stuck on end, and eye shadow and mascara had dribbled round my eyes like a panda. Also, I must have fallen asleep on my face because my nose was flattened out. Who cares though? My nose could spread itself all over my head for all I cared.

I could become just a nose with arms and legs. A walking nose like Vati. No one likes me. I will never have a boyfriend.

Kitchen

I let the cats out because they couldn't be arsed going through the cat flap. They were just sitting in front of the door, looking at the cat flap and yowling. As soon as I opened the door they dashed straight over the wall and into Mr Next Door's fish pond. They always do this. Every morning they go straight to the fish pond and stare into it. They know very well that there are no goldfish in there. They know because it was them who ate them. Do they think that somehow miraculously during the night the Big Pussycat in the Sky made goldfish rain down?

Huh, I'd like to tell them there is no Big Pussycat in the Sky.

In my bedroom
Back in my bed of pain
10:00 a.m.

I have still got my panda make-up on. I like it. I may never wash again. Sounds of life downstairs. Mum called up: "Georgie, we're off swimming. Want to come?"

I didn't even bother replying. Panda Woman does not go swimming. She stays in her room like Lady Havisham in that Dickens book. What is it called? *Crap Expectations*, I think. Anyway, Lady Havisham is getting married but her fiancé doesn't turn up on her wedding day, so she just sits in her wedding dress gathering cobwebs for years and years. Until she accidentally sets fire to herself with a candle. He's a laugh, Charlie Dickens. Not. He should get together with Call-me-Arnold.

Thirty minutes later

They've all gone out. On my own, all aloney. AGAIN.

I know what will happen. The Ace Gang will be ringing all morning and asking me what happened.

Two minutes later

I wonder if he was with Wet Lindsay last night? I can imagine her face on Monday. All full of herself. Swishing her extensions around like a fool. Uurgh. Oh, I can't stand it. I must run away.

One minute later

I could catch the boat train to Paris and live in a garret.

I could cash in all my savings and just go.

Au revoir tout le monde.

Five minutes later

I haven't got any savings. I forgot I bought those cripply shoes that I had to have surgically removed by the doctor.

In Libby's room
Ten minutes later

I hate to do this, but I am desperate. I will have to raid Libby's piggybank. She will forgive me in years to come and know that her big sis had just had enough.

Two minutes later

What sort of mind thinks you put baked beans in a piggybank?

Unless she thinks it's a real piggy. Which she probably does.

Libby's room is like something in a horror film. There are bits of dolls' arms everywhere and hideous piles of pants with lumps in them.

11:00 a.m.

Heard the doorbell ring.

I'm not answering it. It will probably be Mr Next Door saying the cats have got his wife trapped in the greenhouse. Or they have eaten the Prat Poodles.

Or it will be the police because Grandvati has alarmed his neighbours with his surfing outfit.

Anyway, I am not answering it.

11:05 a.m.

Doorbell rang again. Go away.

11:07 a.m.

Doorbell rang again. I'm not answering it.

11:10 a.m.

The phone rang. Oh God, now what?

11:11 a.m.

I suppose it might be one of the Ace Gang. Maybe I should talk to someone about my inner pain. I feel so bored and depressed anyway.

"Hello, Heartbreak Headquarters."

"*Ciao*, Georgia."

It was Masimo! His voice was absolutely gorgey and groovy and mmmmmmmmmmmm.

Mine of course was like a Mousetwitgirl. "Er... *ciao*."

"Georgia, I am... how you say... *mi dispiace*... sorry I didn't call, but last night it got too late... I was... anyway, you are in now."

I tried to sound jolly and full of casualosity. Not like Panda Woman.

"Oh yeah, yeah I'm in now, in as two in things on... holiday in... In land. Hahahahahaha."

Did I just laugh out loud or was I doing brain laughing?

There was a pause and Masimo said, "So, you will let me in, then?"

I said, "Yeah, just ring the bell when you turn up and—"

The doorbell rang.

Oh giddygodspyjamas, he was at the door!!!

I said into the phone, "But I'm not, er... decent."

He laughed. He wasn't laughing on the phone, he was laughing through the door. I could see his outline through the frosted-glass bit.

I would have to speak back to him through the door! But if I could see his shape through the frosted glass, that meant he might be able to see my shape as well. I stepped behind the phone table. I don't know why. I could see my reflection through the hall mirror. *Gott* in *Himmel*, I looked like a Koch – you know, one of the Koch family from my German textbook. In fact, I looked like a Koch who had been adopted by wolves.

I couldn't answer the door like this. I said, "Erm, I'll just have to get dressed."

He laughed again, "OK, but for me you don't have to." And he laughed. "I will wait for you outside. Oh, here are your cats."

I said, "Don't let them near your trousers."

He said, "Er *che*?" But I had bounded upstairs.

Hysteria Headquarters
Two minutes later

Quickly, quickly put something on. Something sexy yet casually morningy. Jeans? Fringey skirt? Jeans or skirt? Skirt or jeans? OH NOOO, I'M NOT GOING THERE AGAIN.

Jeans on and top with "Groove on, groovster" on it? Yes, yes, good, get on with it.

Two minutes later

I didn't have time to cleanse and tone, so I just cleaned up the panda bits and reapplied mascara and lippy. My hand was shaking, so I didn't attempt eyeliner; I would have ended up with noughts and crosses all over my face.

And for the *pièce de résistance* my brain was having a little conversation with itself. Oh good: "Masimo sounded quite relaxed and cheerful, don't you think? Not in a dumping mood." "Yes. And he said that thing when I said I had to get dressed – 'OK, but for me you don't have to.' That was like a display of red-bottomosity, wasn't it?" "Deffo."

Two minutes later

Dashed down to the bathroom. I had the original bombhead. Oh noooo!!! I slicked it down with gel as much as I could. Then I swallowed about half a tube of toothpaste. My nose seemed a bit flat, so I rolled it around in my fingers to give it a bit more shape.

One minute later

Now then just a practice spontaneous smile. Tongue behind teeth and smile. Good good.

Get manic laughing out of system. Hahahahahahahadiha hahaha!!!

And a quick burst of Viking disco inferno to stop the urge to show it to him. Kick kick, stab stab and huddly duddly... HOOORRRNNN!

One minute later

Ready.

Sunglasses?

Good plan.

Sunglasses on.

And open door.

And breathe.

There he was by the gate. His scooter was parked in the street and he was sitting on the seat with his back to me, looking at the kittykats. Mr Across the Road must have been cleaning his car, because there was a bucket of soapy water that Gordy was drinking out of. He had got foam all over his chin. Angus was actually *in* the car lying across the steering wheel. Oh yes, and there was Naomi, her head popping up from the front seat. Mr Across the Road would go ballistic when he found them. But who cares?

I didn't say anything. Partly because I was so nervy, but also because my smile meant I couldn't actually form any words. Masimo must have sensed me being there because he looked round. I nearly fainted. He was wearing a really cool ice blue zip-up top and shades. He took his shades off and in the sunlight his eyes were almost yellow. They were amazing, with really thick curly eyelashes that made him look like he was half asleep. He got off his scooter and walked slowly over to me. He even walks in an Italian way, sort of like slow dancing. He is tall and his hair is a bit longer than the lads here have been wearing it, and it's dark and slightly curly. I had forgotten how fabby-looking he is.

I couldn't move because I had lost all gross motor control.

He kept coming towards me. Maybe he would whip my shades off and say, "Why, Georgia, you are beautiful!" like they do in crap films. Or maybe he would whip my shades off, see my squashy nose properly, and shove the shades back on quickly. Shutup, brain, you are not in this!

After what seemed a zillion years, he was right in front of me. He still didn't say anything. He leaned down to me and I thought, *Sound out the bells of England! He's going to kiss me! Everything is going to be all right!*

He did the taking off of my shades thing, and then he gave me a kiss on one cheek and then the other. What did that mean? It was like a stereo lezzie-auntie kiss!

He said, "Let us go and have a little ride somewhere, *cara*."

I managed to nod. And amazingly my head didn't fall off.

It was a lovely sunny morning and he handed me his spare helmet. I got on the back of the scooter. As he started the engine I was too nervous to touch him, but on the other hand I didn't want to shoot off the back of the scooter when he accelerated away. I put my hands on the back of my seat to hold on, but he said, "Hold on to me." I put my hands on his waist. Just a bit. But he took my hands and put them right round his waist and then accelerated off.

I was so happy to be with him again. He accelerated up the High Street, which was rammed with people. Sadly I didn't see anyone I knew. I wished old Octopussy had seen us. Then we tore down the street and off out of town. I hoped the helmet wouldn't give me the famous Richard III haircut look that is so popular with the criminally insane. I'd worry about that later.

We didn't talk. Well, he said, "Are you all right?" and I did confident nodding until I realised he wouldn't be able to see that unless he was part owl and could turn his head 360 degrees. So I yelled, "Yes, fine!"

Unfortunately, as I spoke, a flying bug flew into my mouth. A really big one, part bug part bat. I nearly choked to death and was trying to spit it out.

Thank God Masimo couldn't see me.

I was coughing and gagging and Masimo said, "What did you say?"

Erlack, erlack, I'd had a bug's bottom in my mouth! But I couldn't say that to a Luuurve God. I finally managed to spit it out and shouted, "I was just singing a song."

He laughed and squeezed my hand. Blimey.

Fifteen minutes later

He pulled up by Downland Woods and helped me off the scooter. I hoped I didn't have bits of bug leg round my mouth, or stuck on to my lip gloss. We left our helmets on the seat and started to walk towards the woods. I walked behind him and did a bit of hair jusshing. Crikey, it was like concrete. My knees were knocking together.

He didn't say anything until we got into the woods, and then he sat down on a fallen tree and sort of patted the space beside him.

Oh, this was fabby and marvy and everything. He was going to snog me. Thank God I had gone easy on the lip gloss. But what if we did that thing where you don't know which side to put your head and you crash heads?

He turned my face towards him and looked right into my eyes and sort of sighed.

Or what if I got Jas disease and had a lip spasm halfway through the snog and had to do pucker release, pucker release? And darty tongue, darty tongue?

Then he kissed me. It was quite a hard kiss and I gripped

on to the log because I didn't want to do my world-famous prat falling off a log act.

Oh, it was so nice to be snogging him again. He put both of his hands on my back and pulled me into him. What were my arms doing just lying there like fools? I thought back to the snogging-lesson days with Whelk Boy. What had he said about arms? Ah, yes, put your hands on his waist. I tried that. Good. The arms were obeying me. Nice work, arms. I don't know how long we were snogging because I didn't have my watch, also my brain had fallen out. I could have easily done it for the rest of my life.

Oh, thank you, Baby Jesus, my prayers have not been in vain. You have not as I thought been too busy to be bothered. I promise I will rescue you from the transvestite world as soon as I get home. And make you new sandals. And a beard.

Eventually Masimo pulled away from me. He gave me a little kiss on the mouth so I had time to recover. He had his hand on the side of my face and he was looking into my eyes. My brain quite literally stopped working. He smiled a really soft, slow smile. Oh, I love him, I love him. He kissed me again softly on the mouth and stroked my hair. (I bet that felt nice with twenty-five pounds of gel on it.)

Then he cleared his throat and said, "Ah, the lovely Georgia, I have missed seeing you. I think you are... how you say... 'mad'. In fact, the Stiff Dylans, they all say, 'Yes, she is mad, that girl.' But they like you. And I like you, very much. Dom told me that you try to get off with his dad and fell through his drum."

Was I going to have to go through this all my life?

Also, that was when I was with Robbie, the boy whose name I will never mention in this life. Anyway, never mind about him, who's name I have forgotten again; this was all good goody good good. I felt like singing, "The hills are alive with the sound of pants." But I didn't.

Then Masimo squeezed my shoulder and stood up. He turned to face me and said, "You asked me – you said you wanted me for you, like how you say in England... to be going out? Is this it?"

Oh yes indeedy, my Pop Star Rock God Luuurve Machine, that is it. He hadn't finished though...

Back in the cake shop of agony

In my bedroom
4:00 p.m.

I'm no longer on the rack of love. I've got off the rack, been to the oven of luuurve, and popped by for a cake from the cake shop of aggers. I'm now lolling in the dustbin of despair. With half-eaten cake all over me.

Masimo said that he doesn't want me to be his girlfriend. He doesn't want anyone to be his girlfriend. He said that it's too soon for him to have a serious relationship with anyone. He would like to still see me, but just like we were before. He said he just wants to have "fun".

Fun.

He said I was "a lovely girl".

Not lovely enough, though, apparently.

I couldn't bear to be with him after he had told me. He put his arm around me and said, "Can we please still see each other? Can I call you?"

I managed to have enough dignitosity to say, "No, I don't think so."

And he said, "I am very sad."

Then for some reason I cheerfully said that I was just popping off to see some friends of mine who lived at the other side of the woods. And I walked off, leaving him there.

After a few minutes I heard his scooter roar off. And I was alone in the woods.

And I didn't have any friends that lived in the forest.

And it took me two hours to walk home. I was so in shock after he had said the bit about not wanting to go out with me that I didn't even notice the two-hour walk home.

There were loads of messages for me when I got in. All from the Ace Gang. Like:

"Phone."

"Double phone with knobs."

And one from Sven: "Oy, missus!!!"

But I couldn't bring myself to ring them back.

5:00 p.m.

Mum brought me a cup of tea. I tried to hide my face when she came in by reading a book, but tears were plopping on to the pages. And it wasn't because the book was *Cinderella*.

Mum said, "Don't worry, the prince comes along in the end, and the shoe..."

But then she realised I was really upset, and she came over and put her arms around me. That made me blub like billio. I told her everything. I said, "He, I (gulp snort), when he came he said... at first I thought he wasn't coming, but he... and then I... to the woods... snogged but I didn't fall off the log... then he said no and I went to visit my forest friends... which I don't have."

Mum told me I would feel better.

I said, "No, I won't."

And she said, "You will."

And I said, "When? In forty years' time, when I am dead? When will I feel better? Today?"

She said, "Well, no, not today."

"This week then?"

"Well, maybe not this week."

"Next week then?"

In the end she said I would feel better "sometime".

It's not much to look forward to, is it?

She asked me if I wanted chish and fipps, but I can't eat anything. My stomach feels as if it's been punched in by twelve very annoyed blokes. And then their mates have come along and jumped on me for a good laugh.

6:30 p.m.

Libby came in to show me her clown shoes. Uncle Eddie has been buying her things from the joke shop. Normally it would have made me laugh, especially as she also had those glasses with eyes that come out on springs. I said, "Not today, Bibbsy. I've got a headache. You have to be quiet."

Amazingly, she did go away, saying, "sssshhhhh" and trying to tiptoe on her enormous shoes. She got out into the hall, still creeping and saying "sssshhhhh", then she closed the door really quietly.

Then she yelled, "Mummmmmeeeeee!!!"

Mum yelled back, "What is it, Bibbs?"

"Ginger's got a headache. FOR CHRIST'S SAKE, SHUT UP!"

Where does she get all this appalling language from?

Fifteen minutes later

I got dressed and went outside into the night. No one would miss me.

8:30 p.m.

I am sitting up the tree in the front garden. Like a dumped owl. My eyes are all swollen up, but I can see into Mr and Mrs Next Door's kitchen window. I wish I couldn't. Mrs Next Door has got a pink flowery winceyette nightie on. Ummm attractive. Mind you, you can't blame her. She is married to the dullest, fattest bloke in the universe (no, not my vati, otherwise that would be bigamy). The Prat Poodles are seated up at the kitchen table, drinking from saucers. How disgusting. AND they have little pyjamas on. Honestly.

Now Mr Next Door has come lumbering in to complete the nightmare scenario. He's got a dressing gown on and you can see his very thin legs – straining to support his vast bottom. They are very very white legs.

More like bean sprouts than legs.

Erlack a pongoes, I nearly fell out of my tree! Mr Next Door isn't wearing ANY pyjamas! He is in the nuddy-pants under his dressing gown! I have been exposed to his nakednosity!! When he picked up one of the Prat Poodles, his dressing gown came apart. I have inadvertently witnessed a porn film.

I quickly changed my position so that I had my back to the Next Doors.

Naomi is on the Across the Roads' wall dragging her bottom along it and mewling. It doesn't seem very romantic, as such, but it is the only way she knows to communicate her love to Angus.

Two minutes later

Well, the mewling and bottom dragging has worked, because here comes the manky tom from up the road. Sniffing around Naomi. Quite literally. And she is not what you would call playing hard to get. Unless you consider lying on your back and sticking your bottom into someone's face playing hard to get.

But that is the harsh reality of life.

Ten minutes later

I wonder what Masimo is doing now. Enjoying himself and his freedom? I bet he's not thinking about me. He probably says that all the girls are lovely. I wonder if he's taken other girls to that wood.

The only thing I can think of that is worse than what I can think of now is if he starts seeing Wet Lindsay. I bet she would agree to anything he said, like, "Will you wear a bag over your head when we go out anywhere?" Which, I must say, I don't think is an unreasonable request.

Five minutes later

I was getting a bit cold and stiff up in the tree, so I thought I would go back into my bed of pain. Just for a change of places to be miserable in. But then I heard voices and Mark Big Gob came by with his mates, otherwise known as the Blunder Boys, and they sat down on our wall under the tree. They were all smoking like ninnies. You know, in that really crap way that boys who are crap do – taking really deep drags and then nearly choking to death. But still talking while they are choking. And talking such rubbish.

Out of the clouds of smoke and over the sound of the coughing I heard Mark Big Gob say, "Yeah, Charlotte with the big knockers was touching her hair well regularly, so I reckon I'm in."

One of the other super-studs said, in between coughing and scratching his acne, "I reckon we could have a foursome with her mate with the spaggy eye."

Are they mad?

Then Junior Mad came along – Oscar. Fabulous news for his parents that he's tagging along with the chavvest blokes in town.

Mark Big Gob said to him, "Want a fag, mate?"

Oh, this should be good. I'd like to see Oscar choking to death.

But he said, "Na fanks, mate, just put one out."

Yeah, in your dreams, Junior Blunder Boy and twit.

Five minutes later

God, I thought listening to Jas rambling on was boring, but she's like Ms Sparkling Personality in Pants compared to this lot. I will never criticise her for talking about voles again.

The lads stopped flicking ash over our garden wall long enough to start talking about a "ruck" they were planning. Nothing like a spot of recreational violence to impress the ladeez.

Then they all did that hitting-hands thing. Why do they do that?

Eventually they larded off and I could get down from the tree.

If this is what boys are really like, then maybe spinsterhood is not such a bad thing.

9:30 p.m.
When I went back into the house it was strangely quiet. I opened the living-room door and saw a horrible, horrible sight. You know when you read about people walking into their homes and there's a cat smeared all over the walls and a bloke with an axe humming to himself in his undercrackers?

Well, it was worse than that.

Mutti and Vati were in the room together.

Alone.

On the sofa.

Near each other.

And Mutti was stroking Vati's beard!!!

Sunday June 26th
9:00 a.m.

I left a note for Mum:

> Dear Mum,
>   Gone to church. I am very upset still and do
> not want to talk to anyone about it. Would
> you answer any calls for me and tell them I
> am out at Grandad's? I will be back for lunch
> but I can't eat anything.
>   Love Georgia
>   p.s. Don't tell Dad anything.
>   p.p.s. If you got that cannelloni stuff from
> Waitrose that I like, I might be able to manage
> that because it's not very chewy.

Walking to church
9:45 a.m.

Well, God cannot say that I do not try. I have fished his only begotten son Baby Jesus out of Libby's toybox and removed the Barbie frock. I couldn't get all of his blusher off, but I have made a replacement foot out of Blu-Tack. He is on top of my dressing table, and even Libby couldn't get up there. And the kittykats would have to erect scaffolding and a pulley to get him down. Mind you, I wouldn't put that past them. Sometimes when they are behind the sofa supposedly purring, I think they are drilling.

The last time I went to God's house, Call-me-Arnold lost his rag with me. Which is a bit un-Christian. After all, there was no real damage done vis-à-vis the elderly pensioner's scarf inferno incident. And it was her fault. And she hurt my shoulder with her handbag and I didn't mention that.

However, as I could be accused of only really chatting to God when I want something, I had better practise humility before I get there. As I walked along, I tried silent inward prayer: "God, you are so big. And omnipotent, not impotent like I once said by mistake. I would just like to say how we're all really impressed down here by your many wonderous deeds. In particular that turning the wine into, oh no, I mean changing the water into the wine thing, and the walking on water. I know that was Baby Jesus, but deep down it is you that is behind it all. I know that. You just don't blow your own trumpet. Not that you couldn't if you wanted to. I bet you can blow anything you like. Forgive me my trespasses and also my dreadful toadying, but you are just so super."

Home again in my room
12:30 p.m.
What a complete waste of time.

And also weird.

The lady organist (who didn't look to me like an ordinary lady, unless you think being six feet tall, wearing a twinset and having four days' growth of beard is ordinary) played a selection of songs from the shows. I don't think the elderly insane who made up most of the congregation noticed, but personally I didn't go to God's house to hear "Chitty Chitty Bang Bang".

And we had to join in the chorus. With actions.

Call-me-Arnold did his sermon seated at our feet on a beanbag. I think it was mostly about ice cream.

Who knows?

Who cares?

I wasn't listening.

Evening

But maybe even the effort of me going to his pad has in some mysterious way made God think I'm not such a bad person, because I have sort of cheered up. Well, not cheered up, I am still miz, but I have decided to look on the positive side as much as I can. Masimo didn't actually say he didn't like me. In fact, he said he did like me. He just doesn't want a girlfriend. That's not my fault; it's just the way it is. Also, Dave likes me, and I have good mates, and I am not a starving African baby. (In fact, I think I have eaten a bit too much cannelloni.)

So I am girding my loins with a firm hand.

Girdey loins

Monday June 27th

Girdey loins. That is my motto for the day.

8:30 a.m.

Speaking of loin girderers, Jas was waiting for me. Her knickers truly in a twist.

She was going, "Well? Well???"

I said, "Well, what?"

"You know, what happened with Masimo? What did he say? I rang about a zillion times."

"I know."

"All the gang phoned you."

"I don't want to talk about it just now; it's all a bit personal."

"He dumped you, then? Well, actually, he couldn't really officially dump you because you weren't officially going out with him. So technically you are not a dumpee. Which is good, pridewise."

What?

Assembly

All the Ace Gang kept looking at me, but I just held myself with great dignitosity. Maybe I held myself a bit too firmly because Ro Ro whispered, "What's the matter with you? Why are you standing like that? Have you been to the poo-parlour division in your knick-knacks?"

No sign of Wet Lindsay, so I haven't had to do pretendy cheeriness yet.

Break

I told the Ace Gang what happened. Everyone was really nice to me. You know, telling me wise stuff and giving advice. Rosie said, "Eat as many of my cheesy snacks as you like." And undid my crisp packet for me and so on.

Everyone was really really good pals to me.

Apart from Elvis, who came whinging along, telling us to

pick up our wrappers and put them in the bins. I said to him, "Just think, Mr Attwood, when you go to that Big Caretaking Home in the Sky, you can collect rubbish all day long. You could build a little shed made entirely out of rubbish and knit clothes made of... "

He went off complaining and moaning.

As I said to Jools, "Even in the middle of my tragicosity, I can still spread a little sunshine into other people's lives."

Blodge

Is it really necessary to schlep all the way to school to learn that we are lugging about 400 different types of bacteria in our tummies?

And that farts are made up of five different gases?

That will be useful when someone lets fly a knee-trembler. We can all sniff deeply and say, "Yes, yes, I think I got distinct tones of sulphur there, with just a hint of baked bean."

Games
Swimming pool

What you have to remember in times of poonosity is that

there is always someone worse off than yourself. I mean, of course, Nauseating P. Green. I don't want to be mean about her, but it has to be said she is very unfortunate looking. And she really does nothing to help herself. In the swimming pool today she was wearing this swimming costume-type thing that was, well, not normal. It was all frilly and had a sort of skirt on it. She jumped in the deep end to ironic applause, and the voluminous skirty-type fiasco filled up with water and she sank without trace.

Whistles were blown, someone set off the fire alarm, and in the mayhem Elvis was hit by a rogue lifebelt. Don't ask me how. Well, you can ask me how. In the excitement of the rescue attempt, Rosie got carried away and started chucking the lifebelts about with gay abandon and *je ne sais quoi*. Elvis, as usual, was in the wrong place at the wrong time. Which incidentally he always is.

How come he is on lifeguard duty for swimming, anyway? I bet he volunteered and Slim was too stupid to understand his pervy tendencies. Serves him right that he got smacked in the face with a bit of rubber tubing. It was only a glancing blow to his hooter but what a fuss he made. And is it all right for a caretaker/pervguard to say "buggering" in front of minors with impressionable minds?

Then the scariest thing in the universe happened. When the sports student had fished Nauseating P. Green up to the surface and was dragging her to the poolside, Miss Stamp ripped off her trackiebums and dived in, yelling, "Keep breathing, Pamela."

As we sat on the side watching them trying to hook Nauseating P. Green out, I said, kindly, "It will take more than four of them to get her out of the pool: the costume alone must weigh four tons."

Rosie said, "Why is Miss Stamp wearing mohair tights?"

She wasn't wearing mohair tights. The mohair tights WERE her legs. I have never seen the orang-utan gene so rampant. If there had been any first formers in the pool they would have been running into the changing rooms scarred for life and yelling, "Run away, run away. It's a manlady, the manlady is coming."

3:00 p.m.
Still no sign of Wet Lindsay.

I'm sort of relieved and worried at the same time.

Where is she?

Maybe she is even now doing ear nuzzling with the Luuurve God. Despite my loins being as girded as is humanly possible, I do feel a bit of a blubbing extravaganza coming on.

4:10 pm.

On my way to late rounders praccy I passed the sports cupboard, and in it were the two little first-form titches I had seen being given a severe ear-bashing by Wet Lindsay. They were sorting out hockey sticks. Astonishingly Dim Monica was there telling them how to do it. Sadly, I think she actually really cares how the hockey sticks are stacked. In a perfect life she would be married to Elvis. (Not the one who dared to rock, the one who should have been hit by a rock.)

As the littlies lugged things around I said to ADM in a casualosity at all times way, "On your own then, Monica? Lindsay got a touch of bubonic plague, I hope?"

ADM said, "Not that it's any business of yours but Lindsay has been to a conference today, so I am taking over her duties. If that's all right with you?"

"Perfectly all right, Monica. I'm sure you will shove

around little first formers as well as the next man."

Home

I've said it before and I will say it again – whacking things about does really calm your nerves down. At rounders practice it did cheer me up to whack the ball and see all the fielders scampering after it like mad bunnies in knickers. Once again, Nauseating P. Green hit the heights comedywise. She has definitely had a bumper bundle day entertainmentwise. I may make her some sort of award. When it was her turn at batting, she hit the ball enthusiastically, missed it, lost her balance, fell backwards, knocking over Katie Steadman the backstop, who then fell backwards into Miss Stamp. It was like watching elephant tenpin bowling (with an elephant as the bowl).

6:30 p.m.

The whole loon contingency is in for once.

Dad said, "This will cheer you up, Georgia."

I looked at Mum, Mum looked at him and gave him her worst look, and he said, "Not... that you have anything to be not... er... cheered up about. But... great news! Maisie has been knitting again! I believe you will find something lovely and thoughtful in your bedroom. For myself, I don't know how I have lived without this." And he stuck his feet in the air. At least they should have been feet, but they were sort of one big sock thing with both his feet in. An enormous footwarmersock in subtle shades of purple and yellow.

Mum had got off lightly with a knitted powder compact holder, or so I thought until she showed me her crochet vest. She said, "I think it's, er, quite... well, I might wear it later."

I said, "Please don't."

She went off laughing into the kitchen. Why is everyone so cheerful? They are probably drunk. Or it's early senility. Marvellous. I'll just be old enough to go and live in my groovy pad in Notting Hill Gate and Mutti and Vati will start being brought home by the police because they've been having a picnic on a traffic island. They will want all their food mashed up. Noooooooooo. Shutup brain.

Anyway I won't care about them when I'm older because I will have given myself to the Lord and will be in a lesbian monastery fiddling with my beards... er, I mean beads.

In my bedroom
Ten minutes later

Oh, lovely. Just what I have always wanted. And so suitable for a long hot summer. How did Grandad's girlfriend know the size of my head to knit me a balaclava?

Five minutes later

She didn't, is the answer.

Also, shouldn't balaclavas normally have a hole in the front where your face looms out? Otherwise, to be frank, what she has knit is not a balaclava, it's a head sock. Still, let no one say that I don't know how to enjoy life.

One minute later

I stumbled down the stairs with my head sock on to show my parents my lovely gift. Mum said, "It's the thought that counts."

And I said, "I know, which is why I'm ringing the authorities right now. Anyone who thinks like she does should be locked up out of harm's way."

When I took the comedy balaclava off, I saw that Mum had her crochet top on. With just her bra under it. The

♡ 149

crochet holes were so big that the whole of one of her nungas stuck out through it. That is how big the holes were.

Dad said, "Cor, Connie, you sexpot," and then lurched to his "foot" and hopped like a fool over to Mum, before crashing on top of her.

How very disgusting.

I went out into the hall to find Libby in her new knitted ear warmers. She had them over her eyes and was saying, "Naaaice and warmy."

Doorbell rang.

Mum said, "Gee, get that, will you? Your dad thinks his back has gone again."

Typico.

I went to the door.

It was Uncle Eddie.

Oh, the fun times just go on and on. His baldy head was glinting in the moonlight and he was dressed from top to toe in leatherette – a lovely look for a boiled egg. He scruffled my hair and said, "Never eat anything bigger than your head." And lurched into the front room to join the other loons.

In the Kitchen

Mutti has just been in to get some *vino tinto* for the elderly loons. She is still wearing her crochet top. I tutted at her and she gave me a kiss on the cheek.

Huh?

One minute later

Miracle of miracles, there is something to eat! Macaroni chiz. Yum yum. Bonkerosity gives me an appetite.

I was scarfing it down when I heard the "music" begin. They are all laughing and cackling in the front room. I know this mood, the next thing it will be... yes, I was right, "Dancing Queen" by Abba.

Why are they so cheerful? Give them a gaily-coloured plastic bag and they'd be beside themselves with happiness. I wonder if I'm adopted. I am so different from them. Vati yelled out, "Georgia, snacks!"

Of course I'm not adopted. Vati is far too lazy to bother with the paperwork.

I was just going to go up to my room when Vati said, "Gee, if you bring snacks I will consider giving you a couple of squids."

Three minutes later

When I came back into the front room with the crisps, I was not amazed to see the horrific sight of Mum sitting on Dad's lap, wearing her prostitute's crochet top – in front of Uncle Eddie. Uncle Eddie was resting his wineglass on his tummy and saying, "I was in the curry shop and the waitress came over to ask me how the biriani was. I was eating my curry and she was practically resting her boobs on my shoulder."

I said, "Oh God, you said 'boobs', that is soooo disgusting!"

Uncle Eddie said, "I only said 'boobs' out of respect for your mother. Normally I say 'tits'."

I went up to my room. I feel physically sick.

My bedroom
8:30 p.m.

What kind of people have an impromptu mid-week vicars-and-tarts party to celebrate the fact that Dad and his mates who play football lost by only ten goals at their last match? My parents, that's who.

Vati burst into my room like a red-faced loon in a dog collar and black tights. Sadly he does in fact look quite a lot like Call-me-Arnold. He was quickly followed by Uncle Eddie, also in black tights and T-shirt. He has drawn a fringe with eye pencil all round his bald head like a mad monk. Good grief.

Uncle Eddie said, "Here's a joke to cheer you up, Gee."

I said, "Father, Uncle Eddie, if you could just go away for ever and be mad somewhere else, that would be lovely. Thank you."

But he just went madly on. "Anyway, this bloke goes up to this house and he's dragging a box behind him. And he says... and he says..."

And then he started laughing and choking so much, I thought I might have to do the Heimlich Manoeuvre, which I am actually in the mood for. Grabbing and shaking someone from behind might get rid of a lot of nervy spasmodosity.

Sadly he recovered himself and went on: "Anyway, he says to the woman who answers the door, 'Are you Mrs Jones the widow?' and she says, 'Well, I'm Mrs Jones but I'm not a widow,' and he says, "Ah, well, you haven't seen what I've got in the box.'"

And then he had to sit down in his extremely snug tights,

he was laughing so much. He will never ever get up again. That is a fact.

10:30 p.m.
The tarts and vicars are in the garden. They've put the loudspeakers outside so that the whole world can enjoy the joy of Status Quo "Down Down, Viva I'm Down."

Five minutes later
Dad has brought out a cake with a huge Roman candle firework in the middle of it.

One minute later
Dad is making a crap speech, which fortunately I can't hear, but I can see his chins wiggling about, so he must think it's funny.

One minute later
Now he's bending over and lighting the Roman candle.

One minute later
Absolutely top!!! Dad has set fire to his own moustache. Blazing!

I think I can sleep easy now. Life does indeed have a bright side.

Tuesday June 28th
In the kitchen

I noticed Dad was clean shaven at breakfast. I said to him, "Vati, what has happened to the little beaver that used to live on the end of your chin?"

But he didn't even bother to reply – just grumped around and went off to "work".

11:00 a.m.

On my way to English I stopped off in the tarts' wardrobe because I had an unexpected piddly-diddly urge. When I came out I saw Lindsay. Octopus head is back. Will we never be free?

She was walking along on her twiglike legs, swishing her naff extensions around. I ignored her but she had something to say: "Georgia Nicolson, well, well, without your silly mates for once. I'm glad that you took my advice about Masimo. I'd like to say you were sadly missed at the club last night, but you weren't. Anyway, we stayed up till way past your bedtime; it was gone nine thirty."

She knows, she knows. Masimo must have told her what happened. Oh, this is sooooo horrible. I don't think I can stand it.

English
In the gym

I can't think of anything except the fact that Lindsay knows about what happened. Miss Wilson wants us to "get in the mood" for *MacUseless*, so we're having yet another workshop fiasco in the gym.

Miss Wilson was rambling on in her sad pinafore dress – yes, pinafore dress – saying, "Oh, this is so exciting. Only days to go till the big night. Come on! Let's get the energy really building. Let's feel that energy, girls!"

While she did that, we all lay down on the gym mats. Or in Rosie's case, hung upside down on the wall bars. Like a bat in frilly black knickers. Mr Attwood will be in in a minute with his perv antenna on high alert.

Miss Wilson was trying to get our attention by clapping. Good luck. She said, "Girls, can I... could I just get you to... er, Rosie, would you mind coming down from the wall bars, and the girls under the vaulting horse, would you just come out now? I want us to begin today's intensive workshop by getting into different characters physically."

I said to Jools, "Lord save us, we aren't going to have to be vegetables again, are we? I'm not in the mood for cabbage dancing, or whatever."

Eventually we all got up and Miss Wilson shouted stuff out and we had to do it. She said, "Macbeth is tortured by his actions. How does that feel? What does it look like? No, Rosie, I don't think that Macbeth would, erm, hang himself with a skipping rope. Can you just put it down now? Right, first of all imagine the weary walk of someone who is feeling very depressed."

Brilliant. Thank you, God. Not.

Ten minutes later

Actually, even though I didn't have to imagine the weary walk of someone who is very depressed, because I WAS someone who was feeling very depressed, I did begin to cheer up at the comedy opportunities of the class. The Ace Gang did marvellous group limping as the Hunchbacks of Notre Dame.

Miss Wilson said, "Very good, girls, but perhaps the person is not crippled, just very depressed. And perhaps depression doesn't always involve so much dribbling. Let your imaginations flow. When I clap my hands and shout out, the next person quickly change into character – and (clap) – now be a happy slender young girl hurrying to meet her boyfriend – and change!"

Oh, the cruelty of life. If God is omniwhatsit, surely he is having a laugh. At me. First a depressed person, now a young girl going off to meet her boyfriend. God pretended he didn't mind about me not rescuing Our Lord from Libby's toy box sooner than I did, but this is his revenge. Nauseating P. Green was skipping round like a fool. If I was her boyfriend that she was skipping to meet, I would have run off quickly to the boyfriend-asylum-seeker's home.

Rosie was doing her famous orang-utan impression. Actually it was very realistic, and it is how she goes off to meet Sven.

Jas had a field day fringe-flicking wise, and actually when she thought I wasn't looking she was puckering and relaxing. And doing a bit of darty tongue. She is still haunted by her lip-spasm fiasco. Ah well, how sad, never mind.

Ellen was still sitting down on a bench dithering about. The bell will have gone before she manages to even set off to meet her imaginary boyfriend. So no change there.

Miss Wilson was encouraging people and walking round showing us what she would look like going to meet her boyfriend (scary, sad and with an alarming smile on her face). Then she said to me, "Georgia, you're still limping. And your back is all hunched over."

Yeah and it's not just on the outside.

Walking home
4:30 p.m.

Talking about the Wet Lindsay nightmare scenario.

Rosie said, "What makes you think that she knows?"

I told them what she said about the club and everything.

Rosie said, "Ah, I see, say no more, say no more, wink wink, nod nod." And started doing the mad nodding-dog thing, and chewing. They were all joining in. I was in the nodding-dog parlour of life.

Jas for once came up with a sort of sensible plan. "Look, I'll ask Tom what's going on." She looked at me from underneath her fringe and did quite a nice smile. "I'll tell

159

him to be, you know, well, not shouty or anything."

I almost kissed her. I said, "Thanks, Jas, you can be a real pally sometimes and I, well, I..."

Rosie noticed I was about to go off on a blubathon and said quickly, "Hey, do you know what book Tarzan wrote? Eh eh?"

We all shook our heads, expecting the worst. And we got it.

"*Lord of the Swings.*"

It was so crap, I must say it did make me laugh. A bit.

Jools said, "Oh, by the way, I meant to tell you Katie Steadman is having another party at the weekend and we are invited."

I don't really feel like parties, but I suppose I have to go on being me.

Friday July 1st
1:00 p.m.

Something unusually good has happened! I think. Maybe.

We normally get made to go out at lunch and freeze around in the grounds while the Hitler Youth (prefects) loll around in the warmey warm inside. So that is why we creep back inside and lurk around the science labs, usually the physics lab, so that if there is a sudden Hitler Youth investigation we can leap into the fume cupboards and pull down the blinds. And crouch there until they go out again. As an additional security measure we crouch down underneath the windows so that we can't be seen from outside. And we heap our science overalls on top of us in case someone comes in and we don't have time to do the leaping-into-the-fume-cupboard scenario, and we can pretend to be a pile of science overalls.

Actually, as it happens, it is absolutely boiling today. At least 180 degrees in the shade.

Ellen said, "Can't we just go outside? Instead of, you know, er, being nearly dying from heat underneath a pile of old overalls… or something."

The rest of the gang started nodding. I had to take a firm grip of the situation. I said, "Yes, yes, of course it would be nice sitting outside in the sunshine, maybe sunbathing and so on… But remember Good Queen Bess – a principal is a principal and we will never give in to the tyrannical ways of… Anyway, everyone under the science overalls. Look natural!"

one minute later

Where was I?

Oh yes, under the window. Which was open. We were just chatting about the wedding. Rosie said, "Sven is wondering what to wear."

I said, "Oh dear. And, anyway, why is he bothering to worry about it? It's never going to happen. Even in five and a half years' time."

Rosie said, "Ah, well, you have always been cynical, Georgia; that is because you have been in the oven of love too many times. But as it happens we are going to have a practice wedding quite soon."

"Don't talk absolute WUBBISH."

Rosie raised her eyebrows at me and said, "So what do you think about flares versus lederhosen?"

We were just about to start discussing flares versus lederhosen when we heard voices and had to shut up sharpish. Especially as we realised it was Wet Lindsay and ADM (Astonishingly Dim Monica). We could hear them clearly, talking outside the open window. We formed ourselves into a convincing pile of science overalls and earwigged.

ADM said, "Well, what did he actually say?"

Wet Lindsay said, "He said that he didn't want to be serious because he had had a relationship before and he was, you know, having a break from serious relationships."

ADM said, "What are you going to do?"

Wet Lindsay said, "Well, of course I'm going to get him to change his mind. The only slight worry is that he started saying that he'd had to upset someone he really liked already, and it sounded like he meant someone here, not in Italy. But he wouldn't say who it was."

ADM said, "Do you have any idea who it is?"

Then Wet Lindsay said the fateful words: "I don't think it can be possible, because she is the most snivelling idiot I have ever come across, but... well... no, it can't be possible. He's not stupid or desperate enough."

ADM went on, "You don't mean... not...?"

Wet Lindsay said, "I know, it would be unbelievable, wouldn't it? But I'm going to keep an eye out, and if I see it's her, well... I just wouldn't be her, that's all."

Then they went off.

Rosie stuck her head out of the overall pile and looked at me. I looked back at her and she gave me the thumbs-down:

"Ohmygiddygodspyjamas, you are dead meat! Deader than the deadest meat in a dead-meat shop!! Give me back your wedding invite. I'll give it to someone who's going to be alive for the wedding."

Emergency Ace Gang meeting
Afternoon break

I said, "Do you think she thinks it's me?"

Jas said, "Well, it's pretty conclusive, isn't it? She said, 'the most snivelling idiot I have ever come across'."

I said, "I didn't know that YOU had been seeing Masimo. Tom the Slug King is going to be very upset."

That shut her up. But it didn't shut me up. "If it is me, then that's quite good in one way because he said he really liked the maybe-it's-me person. Which is really good, isn't it?"

Jools said, "Yes, but what if it isn't you?"

Oh God. What if there are two snivelling idiots that he likes?

Physics

Is it me?

Is he sorry he upset me?

Oh buggeration, I am on the rack of luuurve again. Pass the agony cakes.

Physics is unusually boring today. We are doing statistics. Why?

Rosie wrote me a note: Guess what Slim's vital statistics are: 84, 76, 84 – and that's just the chin area.

I gave her my Klingon salute.

I can't help thinking and thinking about the Wet Lindsay scenario. On the one hand, I am sooooo happy that he might be upset that he upset me, because that would mean he was upset about upsetting me. Which is *bon*. On the negative side, if it is me, Wet Lindsay will kill me.

But even if it is me, it still means that he's not going out with me.

But he might secretly sort of want to.

Five minutes later

I need to make him see that it's me that he wants. I must take advice from the *How to Make Any Twit Fall in Love with You* book and increase my mysteriosity and glaciosity so that he can come pinging back like an elastic band. Maybe if I had a pretendy boyfriend he would get jealous and realise the error of his ways.

Five minutes later
I'll ask Dave the Laugh what he thinks I should do.

One minute later
No, I can't do that because of what he said about the liking business and about messing it up. Also he would start all that Pizza-a-gogo thing again and pretend that Masimo was a girl in disguise and only cared about his hair, etc.

Two minutes later
But in essence, Dave the Laugh likes me.

Two minutes later
And I like him. Dave the Laugh likes me, I like him. What could be more simple pimple?

One minute later
It's not like we're silly children. What's needed here is maturiositiness. Which I have in abundance. Dave and I

could go out together just liking each other. That would be OK. It would be fun.

One minute later
Lots of fun.

Lots and lots of fun.

What's wrong with a boy and a girl who like each other having fun? I like going out. Dave likes going out. We both like having fun.

I can think of all sorts of things we could do. All kinds of places we could go out to.

One minute later
We could go to, oh, I don't know, we could maybe, er... well, for instance, just off the top of my head, er... well, there's a Stiff Dylans gig on in a couple of weeks' time. We could go there for fun.

One minute later
And dance about having fun.

One minute later

Dancing about having fun in front of Masimo – and then see how he likes that!!!

Two minutes later

Oh God, I have once more, in my mind, made Dave the Laugh my decoy duck.

A nip-libbling decoy duck. Who is vair vair good at snogging.

But I would never use Dave like that. Not in a trillion years.

One minute later

He would sus me out, anyway.

One minute later

Unless I was full of subtletosity.

And snogged him to within an inch of his life.

Two minutes later

I have got an internal red bottom that must be struck down. Get thee behind me red bottom!!!

Mad Headquarters
Otherwise Known as MacUseless rehearsals
4:30 p.m.
Miss Wilson gave us her "rousing" rehearsal speech, but Rosie spoiled the effect by burping really loudly. She told Miss Wilson it was "pre-performance gaseous interchange". Let no one say that we don't learn anything in blodge.

Funnily enough, there is no sign of Dave the Laugh. I hope he's not got the lurgy.

Five minutes later
I don't know if it's just me, but there's a mood of hysteria about the company today. Probably because it's only a week to the performance and no one apart from old swotty knickers Jas knows their words properly.

Just as we were having to brief Spotty Norman on taking over on lights for Dave, the door crashed open and he walked in with his tie knotted round his head like a fool.

Miss Wilson started giving him her idea of a bollocking, i.e., "Well, this is really... I mean, it's ten minutes since we started and really it would be nice if you could, erm, be on time."

Dave said, "Time waits for no pants. But I'm here now; let's get this show on the road."

He said hello to his mates and then came over to where I was standing at the side of the stage. I kept my eyes down because I thought he might be able to read my mind and see that I'd been planning to use him as my decoy duck. Actually, he said, "Oy, missus, stop looking at my manly parts."

I tried to have a strop, but he does make me laugh, so I ended up smiling at him.

We started the rehearsal on a high note with the witches scene, "Hubble bubble toil and pants." Rosie in a fit of inspiration stopped stirring the cauldron and segued into a bit of the Viking disco inferno dance. She still had the branch that she used for stirring, but she was free-forming with it. Stab, stab to the right, stab, stab to the left and HOOOORN!

Dave and I burst into spontaneous applause, but Miss Wilson said she was being silly. Rosie said, "I have just introduced a note of Vikingness into the play, Miss Wilson. I think Billy would have liked it."

Miss Wilson was madly doing her buttons up. "Rosie,

Vikings had nothing to do with Shakespeare's *Macbeth*."

Dave said, "Are you sure, Miss Wilson? perhaps Billy didn't tell you everything."

Eventually Miss Wilson managed to get us all back in our positions and on with the play. For a while things were going relatively smoothly. But then it all went downhill. Nauseating P. Green accidentally set off the starting pistol used for the battle scene, and Dave started yelling, "Save yourselves, save yourselves," and racing around. Elvis Attwood came panting up with his fire bucket ready to bury someone in sand should fire break out. He told Nauseating P. Green to mind where she put her bum in future, and stomped off to fiddle with his extinguishers. Miss Wilson managed to get us back onstage again, but then we got to the banquet scene. Now I have to say, in all fairness, none of us really thinks that the juggling and fire-eating improvised scene is a good idea. Melanie is absolutely hopeless at the juggling oranges bit. She more or less just chucks them in the air and they fall all over the place and then she picks them up. It's not as such my idea of juggling. It is actually just chucking oranges about. And as I said to Miss Wilson, "Wouldn't Billy Shakespeare have written it in if he thought it was a good idea?"

Miss Wilson said, "Now, er, that's an interesting point, Georgia, because you see, in Elizabethan times, the play would be, er... well, a sort of moveable feast. The players would take the text and use... well, their own ideas. Like, er... I've had an idea about the juggling and, er, fire and so on."

Rosie said, "Well, what did the Bird of Avon think about your idea?"

Miss Wilson started fiddling with her cardigan buttons. "Well, of course he isn't, well, he couldn't comment on my idea because as you know—"

Dave said, "Was he angry with you because you wouldn't go out with him, Miss?"

Walking home together

The usual suspects. Ellen is going to develop very very strong legs if she keeps on walking home with us. She must be doing an extra ten miles walking a day, such is her luuurve for Dave the Laugh.

Rosie said, "I saw the way Nauseating P. Green was looking at Spotty Norman and I think I could smell romance backstage."

Rollo said, "Sorry about that. I let off during the witches bit."

Jools laughed like a loon on loon tablets. Honestly. Girls can be such divs around boys. Ellen dribbling about Dave, Jools laughing at fart jokes, and Jas hand-in-hand with Tom. Thank goodness I have some pridenosity.

Dave said, "Mr Attwood's a plucky little woman, isn't he?"

Ellen said, "Oh, well, he's not... I mean, he's not a woman."

I looked at her. Dave looked at her. I see no romance made in heaven for her and Dave.

Fifteen minutes later

Just me and Dave. Ellen once again will be nearing home by midnight. She caught the bus at last, still looking moonily after Dave. He gave her a bit of a lazy peck on the cheek and she almost fell over. After she'd gone, he looked at me and went, "What? What?" But he knows what. The sunlight caught his eyes and he looked really, I don't know... maybe it's the time of year, but I think I have slightly got the General Horn. But no no no, mine is not the way of the Horn.

Dave said, "I wouldn't mind being a girl for a day."

I said, "Wow, you mean so you could really know what it feels like to have girly like stuff?"

He looked thoughtful. Dave can be really deep and nice and he is good-looking. Oh blimey, if he tries to snog me, I don't think I've got the power to resist. Then he said, "Yeah, exactly, if I was a girl for a day, I'd just stand in front of a mirror and look at my nungas all day. And feel them whenever I wanted to. S'later, Kittykat."

And he went off quite quickly. How weird. Usually he comes nearly to my house with me, but he didn't. Maybe he's got footie practice or something. Or maybe he's meeting someone. A girl, maybe. A date.

Nearly home
Good. That would be good for him to have a date. Nothing to do with me.

In my room
I wonder who will be at Katie Steadman's party?

Masimo probably won't be there.

Dave will be, though, I should think.

Maybe with his new mystery girlfriend.

I bet she is vair plain.

Mate of the century

Saturday July 2nd
Downtown
Lunchtime

Even though I was not in the mood, the Ace Gang had a spontaneous danceathon outside a record shop. It was playing a really loud song that you could hear in the street, so we thought we'd give the shoppers the benefit of our disco inferno. I think they were impressed, although there was the usual grumbling from the pensioners.

1:30 p.m.

Churchill Square was full of lads all marauding about slapping their hands and fingers and generally acting like prats. One of the prats was looking so hard at our nungas as we passed that he crashed into a shop window.

The theme of Katie's party is "rock".

And no, I don't mean we're all going as striped things with "Blackpool" written down the middle of us. Or boulders.

We have to go as rock chicks and air guitarists and so on. I suppose it will be a laugh and, anyway, I'm not impressing anyone, so who cares what I look like?

Boots

I've got some really dark red lipstick and nail polish and I know Mum will have some ludicrous top I can borrow in lurex or lycra. And I'll wear my three-quarter suede boots.

Evening

In the bedroom of life, tarting myself up for another long evening of goosegogging and silly dancing. But ho hum pig's bum, I mustn't forget that I may well be the person that Masimo likes and doesn't want to upset. Yessss!!! Or possibly noooooo. At least my mates will be there and also Dave the Laugh. You know, in a friendy way that will be nice.

Clock tower
7:00 p.m.

Jools, Mabs, Ellen and Jas were there when I came up the hill. Blimey O'Reilly's trousers, they are all quite literally rock chicks. Everyone is wearing black with just a hint of black. Even Jas has backcombed her hair. Because I will not be snogging anyone tonight, I have been able to risk the boy entrancers. I got some in Boots with the sparkly bits in them. I think they look vair vair cool.

I said to the gang, "Where's Rosie?"

Jools said, "She rang just before I left to say that Sven was having trouble getting his trousers on, so they would meet us at Katie's."

Good grief.

Katie Steadman's house
7:40 p.m.

The house looks quite cool, actually. Katie's got disco lights everywhere, and a boy dressed all in leather (hmmm, that will be nice later on as it's about a million degrees tonight) is at the record decks.

7:45 p.m.

There are fairy lights hung in the trees in the garden! I'm almost beginning to cheer up.

Katie gave us some snacksies and said, "Everyone is going to come – all the lads from sixth-form college, the Foxwood crowd, the St John's boys, er, who else? Oh yeah, the Dame and his mates, and the girls from Moorgrange are bringing mates. I even saw Dom, you know from the Stiff Dylans, and he said they would try and pop by."

She went away and I just stood there. I turned to Jas, who was eating her sausage roll like she hadn't eaten anything for about a fortnight, AND we'd had cheesy snacks on the way here. "Did you hear that, Jas? Did you? Did you? Did you hear that?"

She was chewing and went, "Ummmnff."

"Jas, is that yes or no?"

"Nnfff."

I took it as a yes.

"The Stiff Dylans are coming and do you know what that means? That means that Masimo will be coming, because he's in the Stiff Dylans."

She didn't seem a bit interested, too busy eating her

sausage thing and beaking around, looking at who was there and who they were with and so on. She is very superficial.

I was going to tell the others about the Luuurve God and ask their gang advice when there was the sound of yodelling. Sven had arrived. Crikey, his trousers were the tightest I had ever seen. And he was wearing a fringed cowboy jacket and cowboy hat. Both silver. I don't know what sort of rock bands they have in Lapland, or wherever he comes from, and I don't want to. Rosie was not much better. She had on the tiniest dress and thigh-length boots with shades. (I don't mean the boots had shades; they were not that famous.)

Sven came over to us. "Hello, you wild and sexy chicks. Take me! Use me, you lady animals!!!" And then he picked us up one by one, bent us backwards and kissed us full on the mouth. It is absolutely no use appealing to either him or Rosie. The music started and he went off into one of his alarming dance routines. How he manages to do the splits in those trousers I will never know. It was a very good job that Katie had cleared everything from the room. The leather DJ person looked alarmed. I bet he was hoping he chose records that Sven liked.

8:45 p.m.

The party is really rocking now. Masses of people have arrived. No sign of Masimo or the Stiff Dylans, though. My nerves are shot to pieces. I have to go to the piddly-diddly department about every two seconds. Should I take the boy entrancers off to save any incidents?

Having a breather in the garden
9:30 p.m.

As usual the whole thing has turned into a snogathon.

The Dame arrived with his mates and he made a beeline for me. "Hello, gorgeous, remember me?"

Oh yes, I remembered the Dame. Since I had used my sticky-eyes technique on him at one of Rosie's parties, he was like my slavey boy. I wouldn't mind, but I had only been using him to make Dave the Laugh jealous.

Speaking of which, I wonder where Dave is. Not that I care.

The Dame was looking at my mouth and then let his eyes drift down to my nunga area. Did he really think that was sexy? Then he said, "Do you fancy, you know, coming outside with me?"

180

I said, "We are outside."

Any normal person would have seen the light then, but not the Dame. "Yeah, but do you want to come even more outside?"

Is he mad? I am never using the sticky-eye technique again. I was wondering whether I could just deck him and run when Dave the Laugh appeared at my elbow. He winked at me. "Good evening, sensation seekers."

I've never been so glad to see anyone in my life. I gave him my biggest smile, not even bothering to not let my nose spread out all over my face. I said, "Dave!!! Fabby to see you!"

He looked a bit surprised. "Steady there, soldier. I know I'm gorgeous, but..."

I got hold of his arm and said, "I love this one – let's dance." And I dragged him on to the dance floor.

Half an hour later

I must say I do have a lorra lorra larfs with Dave, and he is a cool dancer. He does this pretend-air-guitar leaping thing that really makes me laugh. We even did a bit of back-to-back air-guitar dancing and lowered ourselves to the floor and back up again. Everyone clapped.

10:40 p.m.

Rosie was holding two drinks in her hands, talking to me about her lovely imaginary wedding. "I think for snacks we'll have a reindeer theme."

Then her "fiancé" came up from behind her and pulled her pants down. Honestly. Her pants were round her ankles and she couldn't pull them up because of her hands being full. Sven went off doing his mad dancing, shouting, "*Oh jah, oh jah!*" his electric-coloured trousers shining on the dance floor.

Rosie said to me, "Take the drinks, ohmygod, ohmygod, quick quick."

But I was laughing too much. I wanted to help her, but it was just too funny.

In the end she had to shuffle over to a table with her undercrackers round her ankles to put the glasses down. Then she pulled her knickers up and went on the warpath to find her "fiancé". Vair funny, actually.

11:00 p.m.

I lost everyone for a moment, and I was so hot from the dancing that I went outside to get some air. I was leaning against the wall when Dave fell out of the French windows. He saw me and said, "It's our song, Kittykat! Let's ROCK!"

He tried to drag me back inside, but I said, "Oh, I can't, I'm too hot, I've got to have a breather."

He said, "Hang on, missus, I'll get us drinks."

He disappeared inside and I could see him grooving his way through the dance floor, stopping to dance with groups of girls as he did. He is such a flirt.

He danced his way back with the drinks and we went and stood against a tree at the bottom of the garden. It was a really lovely summer's evening and I didn't even resent the stars any more. In fact, they reminded me of my night with Masimo. I wondered if the Luuurve God would come. Then I thought that even if he did, it might be quite good for him to see me in the garden with Dave. It might hint at the right amount of glaciosity.

As I drank my drink I looked over the rim of the glass at Dave and he looked back at me. It seemed like ages that we just looked at each other. Then he took the glass out of my hand and put it down on a bench. He took my face in both his hands (I don't mean he ripped it off my neck) and he leaned down and kissed me. He did his nip-libbling thing.

♡

Wow, no one could deny – however much they might luuurve a Luuurve God – that Dave is top at snogging. I was just beginning to get the old jelloid knees and liquid-brain scenario when Dave stopped. No no no not the stopping thing!!!

He said, "Oh no, miss, I am not going through this again." And he lightly smacked my bum and went off into the house.

What? What?

Why did he smack my bum? Why did he stop nip libbling? What does he mean "I'm not going through this again"?

I may be having a spaz attack.

I stayed in the garden for a bit and then went back into the house to find the gang. Sven had taken over the controls of the music station, and the DJ was saying, "Er, could you give me back my equipment, mate?"

Sven put his arm around him. Hmm. Then he kissed the DJ on the lips. I thought Leatherboy was going to throw up. But he has senseless courage, that has to be said, because he wrestled the controls back from Sven. Sven didn't mind, he just stood with his arm around Leatherboy and nodded along to the music.

Jools and Rollo were snogging and dancing at the same time, so they were no use. Jas had gone home early because she wanted to be "fresh" for her ramble with Tom tomorrow. I could see Ellen chatting to Dave the Laugh, so I wouldn't be joining them. I couldn't find Mabs anywhere. She was probably under a pile of coats somewhere snogging. She has very little pridenosity when it comes to having the General Horn.

I went into the kitchen and Ro Ro was in there collecting snacks for Sven. She said, "It's a laugh, isn't it?"

And I said, "Not many, benny."

As she went out, Katie came in and said, "I'm having a groovy time, loads of peeps, aren't there? Really groovy crowd. It's a shame the Dylans couldn't come, but Dom said they had an important meeting."

Oh, typico.

As I came out of the kitchen I saw Dave coming out of the living room with his jacket on. I must have really upset him if he was stropping home. I said to him, "Dave, are you going, maybe I'll..."

And as I said that, Emma Jacobs from St Mary's came out of the room with her coat on. Dave took her hand and said to me, "Yeah, we're quitting the scene, maaan. Stay cool, mate." Emma looked all girly at him, and they went off out into the night.

I didn't want to talk to the others about it, so I thought I'd give Dave and Emma a few minutes and then I would sneak off myself. I felt really really weird.

11:30 p.m.
I am quite literally tossed about on the sea of life.

Up whatsit creek without a paddle.

Or even a canoe.

Why do I feel so weird about Dave going off with someone else? Serves me right because I was only going to use him as a decoy-duckie thing. Except that it wasn't just that, because I really like him, and when I was kissing him I forgot about everything else. Even the fact that I am madly in luuurve with Masimo.

Five minutes later
The streets are really quiet and I can see into lighted houses where people are having indoor fun. And I'm outside on the unfun road.

I am full of confusiosity. Sometimes I feel so desperate, I almost wish I was like Jas. Not in the undercracker-obsession department, but the way she just luuurves Hunky and doesn't think about anyone else. Maybe it's because he really likes her and doesn't like anyone else and that encourages her. Or maybe it's because her mutti and vati are like that. Maybe if she had a prostitute and a madman for parents she wouldn't be so bloody smug and happy. Besides which, she went off home without even coming to find me and see if I was all right. So I am obliged to hate her.

Five minutes later

Dom lives around here somewhere. In fact, I think this is his street. I wonder if he's still going out with that girl? I expect he is; everyone else seems to stay together with people. They are not slaves to the Horn.

One minute later

Ohmygiddygod, there's Dom with his girlfriend! They're sitting on a doorstep. It must be his house. I don't want to let him see me walking home alone. He'll tell Masimo he saw me sadly wandering about like a cloth-eared loon, and that really will be the end of any chance I have for glaciosity and verve. If I walk really slowly backwards they might not notice me, and then I can get round the corner and—

Dom looked up to see me walking backwards. He called out, "Hey, Georgia, what's happening?"

Oh goddygod.

I waved casually. "Hi, Dom... just, just, dropped my er... keys."

What???

Dom got up and said, "Oh no, bummer, hang on, I'll come and help you look. Oh, and Masimo is inside. I'll tell him you're here."

What???

Noooooooo.

I almost screamed at him, "NO... er, I mean, like, don't bother him, I..."

But Dom had already gone inside, followed by his girlfriend, who looked at me in a funny way. I bet she has got girl radar: I bet she knows that I haven't dropped my keys and that I'm just wandering the streets lonely as a clud. Maybe I could hide before they come back? Yes, yes that is it; that's the sensible thing to do. I could just duck down behind a car and they would go away.

Ducked down behind a car
Thirty seconds later

Yes, yes this will work. If I just stay here until they go away, that will be good and fine. Yes yes. Still as a little mouse. I am a small invisible mousey girl.

As I was crouching down a man came by walking his dog. He looked down at me and said, "Are you all right, love?"

And his bloody dog was licking my face.

I said, "Yes, yes, I..."

"Have you lost something?"

"No, er, I mean yes, yes, it's my keys." (Goawaygoaway, stop the licking thing, be gone!)

I heard voices from the other side of the road, and Mr Mad Neighbourly shouted across, "Dominic, there's a young lady here who has lost her keys. Come and have a look, will you? My eyes aren't so good at night."

Good enough to come and spy on perfectly innocent people hiding behind cars, you nosey wally-type person. Why couldn't he be like our neighbours – mad and unhelpful? But, oh no, he had to come HELPING along. What was I going to do?

one minute later

From my position on the ground I could see a lot of legs. This was beyond the Valley of the Very Nearly Quite Tragic and entering the Arena of the It's All Gone Terribly Terribly Wrong.

Then I heard the words, "Georgia? *Ciao. Come stai?*"

Excellent, a Luuurve God has landed.

How does he think I am?

He has dumped me because I am not full of sophisticosity, and now he finds me crouching down behind a car in the middle of the night, with a dog licking my bum.

The only possible thing to do was to look up with a casualosity at all times sort of air about me.

I did. I looked up and smiled and said, "Blimey, Masimo, what a... surprise! Yes, yes, I am, er... fabbio, thanks."

I stood up quickly and said, "Ahahahah! Found them!"

I was deliberately not looking at Masimo. Dom said, "Oh brilliant, where were they?"

"Oh, they must have dropped out of my handbag when I... when I got... when I got my... torch out."

Why did I say that? What kind of person carries a torch with them in a fully-lit street? I'll tell you what kind of person. An imaginary kind of person who is telling enormous porkies. Thank goodness it was night – at least they couldn't see that my whole head was scarlet with just a hint of beetroot.

I risked a glance at Masimo and he was sort of smiling. Does he have to look so gorgey all the time? Then it occurred to me, maybe he thought that I was stalking him, that I'd been hiding behind cars, looking at him. Oh nooo.

I said, "I... er... was at Katie's party."

Dom said, "Oh yeah, shame we couldn't come. Mind you, tight leather jeans are not my best look. But your, er, top is cool."

I looked down at my outfit. Oh excellent, how much like a prostitute did I look lurking around the streets in thigh-length boots and lurex? Happy happy days. I said, "Oh, thanks. Yes, it was a hoot, but it was a bit of a young crowd – you know, silly dancing, that sort of thing – so I took a shortcut home and..."

Masimo still hadn't said anything. But then he said, "Maybe I should walk to your house with you, in case you... lose another thing... maybe your, how do you say in English?"

He said something to Dom in Italian and Dom laughed and said, "Compass."

Oh God, they were laughing at me.

I felt an enormous uncontrollable strop coming on. I was deffo heading for nervy b central, so the best thing I could do was to leave quickly.

I said, "I'll be fine, thank you. I'll just say good night to you both."

Oh brilliant, I was sounding like some twat from Dickens. I was amazed I hadn't said, "And devil take the hindmost."

Masimo touched me softly on the arm. "Come, Georgia, let us walk for a while. *Ciao*, Dom."

Dom said, "*Ciao*," and went off back inside his house.

Two minutes later

We walked along the street in silence. I couldn't remember if I had checked my lippy before I left Katie's. I had left in such a tizz, I hadn't thought to check. Maybe I could just take a little peek now? I could sneak my hand into my bag, feel around for the lippy, unscrew it single handedly in the bag and sneak it up to my mouth while I was looking down.

Or pretend to look behind me and apply it then underneath a pretend cough. No, I daren't risk any more bag movement. Maybe there would be a car mirror? No no, too low. What about a passing bus or lorry mirror? Shutup shutup.

Masimo said, "Did you have a good party?"

I said, "Oh yeah, it was fab and also possibly verging on marv."

Masimo went on (he's got the most amazing voice), "Dom, he say tonight after our meeting that maybe we go to a party for later, but he doesn't say you are there, and I think, maybe I am not in for the party. My mood is not for dancing."

What did "my mood is not for dancing" mean? Did it mean he didn't feel like dancing, or did it mean he wasn't in the MOOD for dancing, i.e., he was in a sad mood. And if he was in a sad mood, what did that mean? Also, he said he didn't know I was there – would he have come if he had known? Or did he mean, he... oh, shut up, brain, shut up. If only he would stop talking and just grab me, that would sort everything out.

Occasionally as we walked along we bumped arms and it was like an electric shock. I really couldn't think of one thing to say, other than, "Snog me, snog me, you gorgeous Italian Luuurve Stallion!"

As we reached my street, Masimo stopped and looked at me. "Georgia, when I last see you, I didn't... well, I want to tell to say, to *spiegare*... to explain about..."

I said quickly, "Oh, there's nothing to explain, you don't have to, I understand."

Masimo touched my arm again. "I think I have hurt you and I didn't... this is not what I wanted. I..."

I smiled my incredibly false smile and said, "Really, honestly, I am fine as two fine things enjoying a fine day out in Fine land."

He looked puzzled. "So, you are saying... you are fine? Everything is all right with you?"

"Yes indeedy."

He smiled at me. "That is good, *cara*. I am happy for that. Now maybe we could be friends and..." Oh no, he had said that word "friends". He got a pen and paper out of his pocket and started writing on it. "Here is my number. Will you ring me, and we can have good times – maybe eat and go for dancing? *Sì?*"

I didn't say anything. I thought I would burst into tears. I just kept the smile on my face. In fact I was smiling so much, I probably would always have to smile because my face was fixed. He put the piece of paper into my hand. I still smiled at him.

Then he bent down and kissed my cheek. "You are so nice. I like you very much, Georgia. Phone me. We can be... how you say here... very good mates. *Ciao*."

And he walked off back up the road. He turned round and waved and blew me a kiss. I waved back, still smiling, singing that old crap song "Smile Though Your Heart is Breaking".

In my room
Just me and the night.

And Angus and Gordy and Libby and her toys.

I don't want to be his "mate".

I've got enough so-called "mates".

Even bloody Dave the Laugh said, "See you, mate."

How come I've gone from "Sex Kitty" to "mate" in less than a day?

I don't want to "have fun" with Masimo.

What does he expect me to do? Go back to his place for a cup of coffee and then say, "Right, I'm off now, see you, mate?"

Five minutes later

Or hang around being a goosegog "mate" while he gets off with other girls at Stiff Dylans gigs. Shouting after him as he goes off with someone, "You chancer! What are you like? See you later, mate. Don't do anything I wouldn't do! That leaves you a lot of scope! Rrrrrrr."

Mate?

I'm not going to be his bloody "mate".

I can hardly be bothered to be "mates" with the "mates" I've got.

I'm already having to be "just mates" with Dave the Laugh.

That's enough "being mates" in anybody's language.

Thirteen minutes later

Mate.

Sunday July 3rd

10:30 a.m.

Jas phoned. "Gee, are you up?"

"No."

"Well, can I come round?"

"Why? Has Tom gone slug hunting by himself? I thought you were going to RAMBLE with him today, and that's why you couldn't be bothered to say goodbye to your besty pal last night."

"Er... no, I just want to see you and chat and do make-up and stuff."

"He's gone slug hunting without you."

"No he hasn't."

"What, then?"

"Well, they've started a Sunday league footie thing and well, you know, it's good for him. And, anyway, he's on a mission because I told him to find out all he can about the Masimo-type scenario."

"Huh."

"What do you mean, huh?"

"I mean huh as in huh."

"Shall I come round?"

"If you like. We can practise being mates, seeing as that's going to be my lifetime achievement award. I'll probably be on TV as 'Mate of the Year'."

Me and Jas in my bed eating cornflakes

12:00 p.m.

Jas thinks it's "fun" at my house. She thinks it's charming that we have mostly biscuits to eat and that my dad sets fire to his beard every other day. And that the cats have been next door and dug up the bones that the Prat Poodles had carefully buried in the compost heap.

And are now chewing them at the bottom of the bed. I can hear the horrible crunching sounds, but I am too tired to care.

It isn't fun at my house.

It's sad.

12:15 p.m.

Jas has just almost made me laugh by getting out of bed and adding a bit to the Viking disco inferno dance. It's sort of sniffing the air. So it goes step to the right, step to the left and then sniff sniff. Like a Viking bison might do. If it was trying to find its prey. And if there was such a thing as a Viking bison.

Excellent.

12:30 p.m.

I am preparing myself to forgive Jas. She has been almost nice to me since she came round. She said that she thinks my nose is shrinking. She spoiled it a bit by adding, "Either that or your head is growing."

Still, it's the thought that counts. Ish.

Is my head really growing?

As we measured it I told her about what happened at Katie's party. I told her about Dave the Laugh going off with Emma and she said, "But you don't mind that because you love the Italian Stallion."

"Yeah, that is clearly a fact but, well, I've known Dave a long time, and he did say that thing about maybe we should sort of be together."

"Yeah, he said that, but what do you think?"

"What do you mean what do I think? How should I know?"

"Well, I know that Tom is my one and only one."

"Yeah, but that is because you are so boring, er, I mean too, er... you are too blind with luuurve to hear the call of the Cosmic Horn."

"I know."

She is sooooo annoying, but I suppose she is just being her.

Because we were being so cosy and back to the old days of besties, I bared my whatsits to her. I told her about walking home and bumping into Masimo as I was having my bum-oley licked by a dog.

She said, "Oh blimey, mate."

She had said the "mate" word, but I let her off.

She went on: "So, are you going to give up on him now then?"

I said, "Yep, I tried the girding of the loins scenario, however my loins came ungirded. Which can be quite painful, especially if you're wearing tight jeans."

We had a bit of a laughing attack for a bit because it has to be said, even if no one except me will say it, that I am despite being sheer desperadoes and in the cake shop of aggers, etc., quite a good laugh.

When we had built up our energy with another packet of Wotsits, I went on: "I'm going to have to think that he doesn't exist and *ignorez-vous* him."

"So when we go to the Stiff Dylans gig will you pretend he is a figment of a sham?"

"No, I will not pretend he is a figment of a sham. I won't have to, and do you know why? Because I won't be going to the next Stiff Dylans gig."

"Blimey."

I nodded while I crunched through my Wotsits.

"That is a fact that is written in stone. I will NEVER be going to a Stiff Dylans gig again."

"Blimey."

"He gave me his phone number and told me to call so that we could go out and do mates-type stuff."

"Blimey."

"Jas, will you think of something else to say besides blimey, please?"

"OK."

"But I will tell you what I'm going to do with his telephone number. I'm going to go into the woods and ceremoniously burn it so that I will never be tempted to call him even in my darkest moments of jelloidnosity."

Jas started to say, "Blim... er... crikey."

In the woods
3:00 p.m.

I have burned the paper with Masimo's number on it and buried it under an oak tree. (Well, Jas scraped away a bit of soil with a twig she found and we covered it with that. And it took her long enough to do that because she found a mushroom that she thought might be a "special" mushroom.)

9:00 p.m.

I don't even feel tragicostnosity. I feel nothingnosity.

Which is not easy to say, believe me – tragicostnosity in particular.

However, I will never feel anything again.

Good.

I am done with love.

It's a mug's game.

I am just going to sit in my room for the rest of my life not doing stuff.

10:00 p.m.

How boring is this?

It's as boring as double maths followed by a lecture from Slim on how life was when she was a girl and used to go to Sad Girls High with Queen Elizabeth and Tom Thumb, or whoever was lurking about boring the arse off people in those days.

10:10 p.m.

Got out my letters from the ex Sex God. I don't know why I keep them. Or the photos of him. Just to torture myself. I should throw them away with the rest of my life.

I will put all the things I have of his together and do that thing you're supposed to do when you are moving on in life – burn them to ashes and smithereens and never look back. Out with the old and in with the new lesbian monastic life.

10:15 p.m.

Robbie wrote: *It would be really nice to hear from you. I often think about you.* Well, that's nice, isn't it? In a way. At least he hasn't mentioned the word "mate".

10:30 p.m.

Maybe I'll drop him a line. Perhaps he'd like to hear from a lesbian monk. Who wouldn't?

10:35 p.m.

What harm can it do, anyway? He is miles away – he's over the Trans-Siberian Ocean, or whatever it is. In the land of rogue bores and exploding whatsits.

10:45 p.m.

What shall I say? I must tread a fine line between glaciosity and friendlinosity. With just a hint of "you don't know what you are missing, my fine feathered friend".

Midnight

It was quite hard to write the letter. But in my new mood of baring my all – oo-er – I told him everything. I thought, *Oh sod it! Devil take the hindmost! Take me as I am, the real Georgia. The real true person, no longer afraid to stand tall and proud. Burned in the oven of love and fattened in the cake shop of agony and...* Anyway, what was I saying? Before I wandered off into the cake-shop thing again?

Ah, yes, honestosity.

12:03 a.m.

Obviously I left out the bits about me making a complete and utter pratty baboon of myself. I told him all about the bison horns and the Viking wedding. I even mentioned that Herr Kamyer might be matron of honour.

12:05 a.m.

Actually it has quite cheered me up writing it all down. It doesn't seem like such a bad life when you think of the hours of fun the Ace Gang have had despite the Hitler Youth, parents, the orang-utan gene, lurking lurkers and so on.

I couldn't help myself adding a few details about Wet Lindsay and her astonishing stick-like existence. I thought it was a mistress stroke of seemingly nicenosity to say about her: I expect you know that Lindsay is head girl and she is making a very good job of it; some of the first formers may never go out on their own again. Also, she has once again put herself at the forefront of fashion vis-à-vis her interesting hair extensions. That kind of courage is rarely seen outside the circus these days.

I sort of skated around the boy issue. I mentioned the Stiff Dylans in passing because it would have seemed odd not to. But I just said: I've been to a few gigs, which have been quite good. They have a new singer called, erm, I think it's Masingo or something. He seems quite nice, but may be a froggy-type person. I saw Dom's vati and he seems to have forgotten about the time he thought I was trying to get off with him because I thought he was a

♥ 205

famous music-agent-type person. Speaking of vatis, my own portly one set fire to his beard, so no change there.

I had sort of lost all inhibitions by then. It was quite a relief to tell a boy everything (more or less), and what had I to lose? I didn't have to impress him any more.

12:07 a.m.

I didn't know how to end it. Was "with love" all right?

I am certainly not going to put "from your mate".

Finally I decided on: Well, I'm away laughing on a fast camel now. It would be great to see you again. Take care. Love, Georgia.

And I put a kiss.

But I thought that might be construed as a bit on the matey side, so I added two more.

Three kisses.

That's OK.

It doesn't imply rampant red-bottomosity. It implies *je ne sais quoi* with a hint of longing.

12:10 a.m.

But he probably has a girlfriend called Gayleen.

Or Noelene or Joelene.

Who is a wombat.

Monday July 4th
On the way to Stalag 14
8:20 a.m.

I am wearing a black armband because this is the day that the Hamburgese chucked all our teabags into the sea and said they didn't want us to rule them any more.

That is when they started making up their own language, and see where that's got them.

It's got them into the restroom of life.

And had them wearing panties instead of proper knickers.

But let them have it their way.

Let them wrap themselves in aluuuuuminum as much as they want.

We in Billy Shakespeare land do not hold grudges and will love them always.

Until they get more sense and let us rule them again.

♡ 207

8:30 a.m.

Met Jas at her gate and she did immediate armsies-linksies, which is nice. But I didn't let on.

I said to Jas, "Mum's the word."

She looked at me. "Why are you talking about your mutti?"

"NO, Jas, I mean that you mustn't say anything about the party and the Dave the Laugh scenario or me being Masimo's 'mate'."

"I know when to keep my mouth shut."

"Wrong."

8:35 a.m.

When we got to the postbox at the bottom of the hill leading to "school" I wondered if I should post my letter to the Sex God? Hmmm. I asked Jas, which is a terrible mistake. She said, "I thought that you loved either Masimo or Dave the Laugh, and now you're writing to Robbie."

"I know that."

"You are sort of three-timing except that none of them are your boyfriend."

"Shut up, Jas, you are not Baby Jesus."

"I know, I'm just saying that Baby Jesus will be very disappointed with you."

"No, he won't. He will luuurve me no matter what I do, and by the way, whatever I do is bound to be more interesting to him than what you do, O Voley One. Hey, Jas, don't be volier than thou! Hahahaha, Jesus will like that one; it's a religious/wildlife joke! I think I might be hysterical. What shall I do? Help me, little Jazzy, shall I post it or not?"

She looked thoughtful, which is always alarming, and then she said, "Well, let's use logic. If we see a white van in a minute, you should post it. But if the white van has a bloke with a baseball cap on, you should wait until this afternoon to post it, and if..."

8:40 a.m.

Saved the trouble of whether I should post the letter or not by a fantastically insane and grumpy postman who came along to empty the postbox. He just tore the letter out of my hand and put it in his bag. I said, "Erm, I haven't quite decided whether I wanted to post that or not."

He just said, "Bog off to school."

That's nice, isn't it? As I have said to anyone who will listen (i.e., no one), the point about public servants is that they should serve the public, i.e., me. But they just don't get it.

2:00 p.m.
Forty-five years of being cooped up at Stalag 14, interrupted by only two Jammy Dodger breaks.

Should I have posted the letter?

2:30 p.m.
What does it matter, anyway? With my luck it will either not get there, or he will not bother to reply, and then I will have been rejected by practically every man on the planet.

2:35 p.m.
That's it, I'm going to concentrate on my career. I may as well become a multi-lingual lesbian monk.

In the corridor, lolloping along to French
2:55 p.m.
I am keeping mum as two short mums, even though the Ace

Gang has been asking me what is going on vis-à-vis romance. When I said to Rosie, "Nothing has happened. There is zero to report," she just looked at me like a looking-at-me thing. But I didn't snap.

I would have been extremely good at being in the French Resistance during the war if anyone had bothered to ask me.

Which they didn't.

And even if I had been alive, I wouldn't have said yes because of that business of the French saying the English were a bunch of cheese-eating surrender monkeys.

Or did we say that about them?

Oh, I don't know. Stop asking me trick questions.

3:00 p.m.

By mistake I have overdone things and actually handed my French homework in on time. I thought Madame Slack was going to have an f.t. but she didn't, more's the pity. She just said, "Who did you copy this from?"

Which I think does little for student-teacher relationships in these troubled times.

For once in my whole school life I'm walking home on my own. I told the Ace Gang that I had to dash for a doctor's appointment, but I haven't really. Although if Mum had her way I would spend every waking hour in Dr Clooney's surgery so she could moon around him. It's just that I couldn't handle the risk that Dave the Laugh would come along and I would have to walk along with him and his mates as if everything were in Norman Normal land. I don't know why I don't want to see him. I just feel funny about him and Emma Jacobs.

I'm not the only one, either; Ellen practically had a nervy b. about it. At break at Ace Gang Headquarters she started talking about him going home with Emma Jacobs and going, "How... and why... why???" She had a full-blown head-shaking ditherama.

I had to practise extreme glaciosity and also extravagant bursts of manic Viking disco dancing just to stop the Ace Gang asking me why I left early and if anything happened to upset me and how I am feeling, etc.

But it is my own painful little secret not to be shared. The only person who knows anything is Mrs Big Pantaloonies.

Five minutes later
And I have told Radio Jas that she is sworn to secrecy.

One minute later
So the Ace Gang will know everything that happened by now.

One minute later
And also possibly how many times I have been to the loo in the last day.

Five minutes later
As I went down the hill I saw the two little titches from the first form, who had been duffed up by Wet Lindsay, hopping along. And I do mean hopping. Did I used to hop when I was their age? Surely not. As I passed them they looked exhausted, hopping along on one leg with their big heavy satchels. I suppose I have on occasion pretended to be riding a horse home, but not carrying a big heavy bag.

Life is a mystery.

Lesbian Monastery Training Headquarters, aka, my bedroom

Evening

I will dedicate myself to the pursuit of knowledge...

zzzzzzzzzzz.

MacPants

Wednesday July 6th
Afternoon break

Fortunately the Ace Gang has gone on to more interesting subjects than me. They are concentrating on the Rosie-Sven Viking wedding with gusto. Rosie said, "I have an idea for a lovely outfit for Sven. I will gather the materials on Friday at the *MacUseless* dress rehearsal."

She wouldn't go any further, except to say that Sven will be "thrilled".

And none of us really want to see that.

4:30 p.m.

Walking home with just little Jazzy Spazzy, who is muttering her Lady MacUseless lines to herself. I hope she isn't turning into a spasmodic or whatever it is when a person is two people at the same time.

I feel a bit nervy about seeing Dave again on Friday. I'm going to have to practise this "mate" malarkey with gusto. And possibly vim. What would a mate do when they saw their mate? What do I do when I see my mates?

Three minutes later
In Jas's case I will tell you what I'll do in a minute if she doesn't stop rambling on about spots.

Five minutes later
Unfortunately I said what was in my head out loud. "Jas, if you don't stop rambling on about spots, I will have to kill you."

Jas stopped mumbling, "Out damned spot!" and said, "Don't pick on me because you have got the Cosmic Horn for any boy that comes along, but they just want to be mates with you."

Fifteen minutes later
Here is my recipe for a mood enhancer: take a friend, preferably one with a really annoying fringe and outsize pants, and when she's rambling on, swiftly push her into a

216

ditch and run away.

Hahahaha.

Very funny to see Jazzy Spazzy plunging down the grass verge.

Hahahaha.

Friday July 8th
MacUseless Headquarters
4:50 p.m.

Dress rehearsal in front of the whole school at 5:30 p.m.

Tension mounts. It's showtime, showtime...

zzzzzzzzzzzzzzzzzzzzzzz.

Miss Wilson gave us her world-famous pep talk, but we still managed to stay awake. Apparently the honour of the school is on our shoulders. We have two nights of parading around in tights yelling "och aye" to persuade everyone that going to school is not a complete waste of everyone's time. And just an excuse for people who would have nothing else to do, i.e., Hawkeye, Slim, Madame Slack, Herr Kamyer and the terminally insane Elvis Attwood, to go somewhere and not bother people on the street.

Thankfully we have Miss Wilson steady at the helm, so everything should be, you know, a shambles.

Jas was watching me like that mad Red Indian bloke in the film about Mohicans – Chingachgook. He trailed around in a feather hat, following bison poo and watching people. Jas hasn't spoken to me for two days because of the accidental grass-verge scenario. But she was really looking at me in a horrible beaky way when Dave the Laugh came in with the other lads.

5:00 p.m.

I kept a safe distance from Dave, but not so much that he would notice and think I was avoiding him. I stuck around with Ro Ro and Jools and the Ace Gang. Nauseating P. Green kept coming up to me for reassurance and asking me if my sword was comfortable. She actually believes that I am her husband, which is possibly the most tragic thing that has happened to me. And that is saying A LOT.

Still, no one can say that I'm not a taking-it-on-the-chin sort of a person. And believe me, I have taken it on the chin A LOT. I hope that my brain will stop saying A LOT soon. And I mean that A LOT.

Only half an hour to go till curtain up. Although as Spotty Norman is in charge of curtains, I have hope that this production will quite literally never see the light of day.

I had been busy in "make-up" with Ro Ro until Miss Stamp (And what has this production got to do with her? Is there a lesbian sports bit? Possibly, actually, as I haven't been arsed to see the whole play through, only my bits.) came in and took charge of the fake fur. Rosie was forced to remove her moustache, which actually was a homage to Miss Stamp in the first place.

I was doing my limbering-up exercises with Rosie, i.e., horn to the right, horn to the left, when Dave the Laugh passed close by, winking and lumbering bits of castle wall and so on. Fortunately, I had three foot of foundation on, so he couldn't have seen my vair vair red face. As he went by, I burst into peals of laughter as Jools handed me her witch's branch. Dave looked at me. Jools looked at me. Which was fair enough, as all she had said was, "Will you hold this while I go to the piddly-diddly department?"

Not exactly a joke.

But I wanted to let Dave know that I was fine and not bothered about the snoggus interruptus that we had done at

♡ 219

Katie's party. And also that I didn't give two short flying pigs' bums about who or what he went out with.

Ellen was also giving him her version of the cold shoulder. Which was hilarious. She said to me, "I'm going to let Dave know exactly what I think of his behaviour. I mean, that is what I'm going to do. I should do that, shouldn't I? I mean, do you think I should? Because I think that's what you should do – you should... anyway, what do you think?"

Oh dear Lord.

She shouldn't have bothered because her cold shoulderosity only lasted two minutes. Dave came by covered in twigs, saying, "Do you think my acting is a bit wooden, girls?" Ellen went bright red and giggled like a loon. Not exactly in my book tip-top cold shoulderosity work.

Moi, on the other hand, did an excellent job. I slightly-smiled in a way that meant I was an amusing sort of person, but not the sort of girl who really bothered what Dave the Laugh got up to.

5:50 p.m.
Jas brushed past me in her frock to go poncing around as Mrs MacUseless. I smiled in an attractive way, but she

*ignorez-vous*ed me. She'll come round; what other fool will listen to her talking about voles? I'm not on for a bit, so Rosie and I went back into the props box for a rummage. Oo-er.

Rosie pulled out a false nose and said, "Do you think if I put it on as a sort of two-nose effect anyone would notice?"

I thought back to the good old days of last year. Days when life had been so simple. I had luuurved the Sex God and been his nearly girlfriend. We were doing a production of *Peter Pan*, and like now, many fools were stropping around in tights. (Apart from Nauseating P. Green, who was a dog.) Rosie and I had been banned from the production and put on props. We found some theatrical fur, and every time we handed a sword or something to Wet Lindsay onstage, we would add more fur to our bodies. By the end of the show we had huge, furry hands and Rosie had one massive eyebrow and sidies. How we laughed our way to triple detention. Happy happy pre-spinsterhood days.

That's when Ro Ro said from upside down in the props box, "I am going to secrete this fur about my person and take it home for the Viking wedding."

It's pointless under those sort of circumstances (i.e., Rosie being utterly barking mad) to ask questions.

8:30 p.m.

Some fools actually applauded at the end as we took our bows. I only had one unfortunate incident doing my part, but I don't think anyone noticed.

Walking home with the gang
9:10 p.m.

Jas is keeping up her humpiness by walking as far away from me as possible. And she gave everyone except me one of her secret Midget Gem selection. I don't care because I think she keeps them hidden in her enormous pantaloonies.

Then in the distance we saw Dave the Laugh and his posse following behind us. Donner *und* Blitzen. I was going to *ignorez-vous* them with a firm hand.

I said, "My false beard fell off when I was doing the swordfight and I had to carry on one-handed while casually holding my beard on with the other one. Did you notice?"

And Ro Ro said, "Yes, who didn't? It made you look like

Mincing Macduff, the campest bloke in Och Aye land."

Excellent.

Not.

9:15 p.m.

Dave and his posse are doing comedy fast walking to keep up with us. They'll catch us up in a minute. Oh, I can't handle any more of this "mate" business. I said to the gang, "I fancy a bit of a run, actually, so I think I'll just go on ahead. See you for the final fiasco performance tomorrow."

They looked at me in amazement as I jogged off. After a minute of jogging I looked back and Dave the Laugh was also now jogging. Oh nooooo. I put on a bit of speed, but he caught up with me and just jogged along beside me, looking at me. He was looking basooma-wards and I didn't have my double strength over-the-shoulder-boulder-holder on. Drat and double dratty drat.

Still jogging
Two minutes later

This was ridiculous. As we jogged on side by side Dave put his arm through mine, so we were doing tandem jogging.

♡

Eventually the weight of my basoomas got the better of me and I slowed down.

Dave said, "Have you got the hump with me, Kittykat?"

I turned to him, and in between panting smiled a really really beaming smile. "Dave, why on earth would I have the hump with you?"

He looked at me. "You have got the hump then."

Damn.

He went on, "You know that you don't want to go out with me and so I'm going out with someone else. That is OK, isn't it? Or would you just like me to sort of hang around on my own for ever just in case you feel like a quick snog?"

Actually, when he put it like that, I thought, *Yep, that is exactly what I would like.* But it didn't seem a very normal thing to say.

I was trying to think of what was a normal thing to say, which quite honestly I have never really had a proper education in – nothing my parents have ever said would pass for normal conversation. Anyway, as I was just flicking through my brain for something normalish to say, my brain went off for a little holiday to Hornland. I started thinking about the way Dave's eyelashes curl up and his mouth goes sort of down at the corners and how... And that's when he gave me a quick kiss on the cheek and went off back to his mates.

Bugger.

Midnight

So this is my fabulous night: my beard fell off and Dave the Laugh saw my basoomas unleashed.

And he is definitely going out with Emma.

Which I don't care about.

Much.

Ten minutes past midnight

I have decided to use art to express myself. Tomorrow night I will give the performance of my life. My part is mostly blubbing and fighting, and God knows I've had enough practice at that.

I will let Dave see that I can be as full of maturiosity and sophisticosity as the next fool.

Saturday July 9th

Even though I tried to give them the wrong date, my mutti and vati, grandvati and Maisie are all coming to the performance tonight.

7:00 p.m.

I've got about four tons of glue on my beard. With my luck, it won't come off at the end of the show and I will have to go immediately to the lesbian monastery.

7:05 p.m.

Backstage is a nightmare of tights. Jas is wandering around with her bloody dagger, muttering her lines to herself. It is very unnerving. She was saying, "Unsex me here and fill me from the crown to the toe top-full of direst cruelty... Is this a dagger which I see before me...?"

And then doing manic stabbing.

Like a loon.

Which she is.

I must remember never to fall out with her if she's cutting up sandwiches.

It's not likely I'll have the opportunity of falling out

with her as she is still *ignorez-vous*ing me.

7:30 p.m.
Curtain up, amazingly. I can see through a crack in the screens at the side of the stage and the hall is packed. Oh brilliant. My "family" are on the front row.

The banquet scene
8:30 p.m.
Everything not going too badly.

Apart from Dave messing up the sound effects. The banquet scene, which should have started off with bagpipe music, had seagulls instead. Which must have puzzled the audience a bit.

But then, after Jas and her "husband" Honour Stevens (also known as MacUseless the Thane of Cawdor) ponced around with their soon-to-be-dead guests, the improvised entertainment scene began. God knows we had all tried to advise Miss Wilson against the juggling and fire stuff, but would she listen? No. Melanie was doing her best with the oranges, flinging them around and dropping them and so on. She was being put off even more by ogling oglers (the

Foxwood lads) all crowded on the side of the stage, desperate for a bit of nunga-nunga jiggling. So oranges were crashing around, left, right and akimbo. And I distinctly heard my grandad say, "She's a big girl."

But the *pièce de* whatsit was Ellen on fire-conjuring duties. Anyone who thinks it is sensible to give fire to someone as divvy as Ellen has to go to a home, frankly. Anyway, Ellen had some special paper that you light and it whooshes up and it looks like you've set fire to your hands. But you haven't really. You just whoosh the fire about (or your flaming hands, as the audience thinks) and eventually the paper burns up and disappears into the air with no harm done. That is the whooshing-fire theory. And last night the whooshing had been without incident.

Credit where credit is due, Ellen lit the paper and did the initial whooshing of the hand with no lack a day or incident. But then she whooshed too near to Spotty Norman and his false beard, and the rest is history. Actually, Spotty Norman was almost history. As his beard flared up, Norm came offstage, shuffling sideways quite quickly. It was Elvis's moment of triumph. He appeared like Mr Mad the fireman with his fire extinguisher, and gave Spotty Norman and Nauseating P. Green, who happened to be standing nearby, a good dousing with foam. The beard was extinguished, but Norman and P. Green blundered around like blind blundering things for about five minutes.

Vair funny.

9:30 P.M.

We were at the big fight scene when Great Birnam wood comes to High Dunsinane. Everyone was dressed up as trees, etc., and as I said to Rosie, "Oh, it's a triumph, darling, a triumph lovie."

And it was, until Dave the Laugh, master technician and fool, struck.

I really thought Miss Wilson had lost her grip and would have to be airlifted to a secure unit. She had a complete and utter nervy tiz when Dave (on lights) plunged everything, not only the stage, but backstage, frontstage, sidestage, into complete darkness.

Most of the forest fell off the stage. I was at the side of the stage when he did it, and in the pitch black I felt a hand pinch my bum. OY!!!

I am convinced it was Dave, but when the lights went on

again he was just looking really surprised and going "What? What?" to everyone. He said that he had "fallen" against the light switch accidentally.

The audience applauded the Forest Folk plunging into the audience! They thought it was part of the modern interpretation, which just goes to show what fools parents are on the whole.

9:45 P.M.

Even if I say it myself, I was magnifico as Macduff. I actually blubbed real tears, and that wasn't very hard, given my life. As I came off the stage I sneaked a look at the audience, and even Hawkeye looked a bit wet round the eyes. Dave the Laugh gave me a hug as I went by and said, "Well done, Kittykat. You are a thespian of the first water and also your nungas look particularly perky in that tunic."

Oooh, he is soooooo aggravating.

9:55 P.M.

We got a standing ovation. Well, from those of the audience who could stand. I noticed Grandvati only managed to get to his feet at the same time as everyone else was sitting back down.

10:20 p.m.

Hoooray!!! Slim declared an armistice because of our vair vair marvy performance. She gave me and the Ace Gang our horns back!!!

We did a little celebration Viking disco inferno dance, but I don't think she got it. She just jelloided off to chat to the elderly insane.

Mr Attwood looked like he thought he was going to get a medal for his firefighting skills. He was going on and on to anyone who would listen, "Yes, luckily I've been practising for just such an emergency as this. I have a stuffed figure in my allotment which I regularly set fire to, and I've got my extinguishing time down to ten seconds."

Good grief, what a fabulous life he leads.

I say we all did a little Viking disco inferno dance, but Jas didn't. She is still sulking. I heard her say to Jools that she was exhausted from all of the emotion she'd put into her part. I don't see why – she only stabbed someone and then went on about a spot. Anyway, she left before us, snuggled up to her boyfriend. She was leaning against him as if she was a paralysed elf. It's pathetic. She said goodbye to everyone except me.

She won't be able to ignore me for ever.

I refused to get in the batmobile with my parents. Vati said, "Don't you want to accelerate through the night in my Lovemobile?"

Urgh, good Lord. And he said it in front of everyone. And he is wearing a T-shirt and tight jeans. Is there a book called, *How to Be Really Crap*, because if there is, he has got it.

Grandvati insisted on showing the gang his false teeth before we could bundle him on to the bus with his almost completely knitted girlfriend. Even her handbag was knitted. And her purse.

Midnight

When I got in, Mutti had made me a special supper and Libby had decorated my bed. Well, what I mean is she had her dressing-up fairy clothes on and had put tinsel on all her "fwends". And I do mean all her fwends – scuba-diving Barbie, Charlie Horse, Pantalitzer doll's head (which is all there is left of her since Gordy had a spaz attack and ripped her arms off), plus various bits of vegetables. They were all crowded in my bed, waiting for me in a really scary way.

Especially as the light was off, and when I turned it on there they all were in the bed. Libby shouted, "Heggo, Gingey, SURPRISE!!!"

You're not kidding. Even Gordy and Angus and Naomi were in there, tied in a shopping bag so that they couldn't escape.

You try getting your jimjams on with a toddler in wings clinging to your leg.

It's not easy.

But what is?

Sunday July 10th
1:30 p.m.

Let me just say this – never go to the park with a toddler round your waist.

Libby will not leave me alone.

2:00 p.m.

In the end I got up my private tree again just to escape from her. I have got post-performance exhaustosity. If I could just wedge my bum into the bit between two branches I could have a little zizz.

Fat chance. The kittykats are messing about in Mr Next Door's pine tree doing that all-legs-at-the-same-time climbing thing up the trunk. I shouted to them, "Oy, you two, get down. Don't you dare go up that tree!" And I threw stuff at them.

It worked, actually. They both stopped and lay on a branch and looked down at me, yawning. They did a bit of light bum-oley grooming, and then went back to the all-legs-at-the-same-time climbing.

Then I heard a scooter engine in the distance getting nearer and nearer. And it was him – Masimo on his scooter! On the bottom road coming towards my street! Wow!! I wonder if he'd heard about my outstanding Macduff performance? Shutupshutup.

Oh God, how am I going to get out of the tree without him seeing me? Actually, I think my bum is stuck. Oh brilliant. And I don't have my lippy on. Oh *merde, merde, merde, merde*! What should I do?

Maybe it's just a "mate's" visit?

At which point Masimo rode right by the bottom of my street without stopping.

Of course he did.

That is my life.

2:30 p.m.

Oh, excellent day. Really, really excellent in every way. I am on the rack of love again eating aggy cakes – with my bum wedged into a tree.

Four minutes later

I've unwedged myself, but I think I've bruised my bum-oley.

Walking up the garden path in a very odd way

I think my bottom's swelling up.

Five minutes later

For the *pièce de résistance* the kittykats really *are* stuck up the pine tree next door. At the top of it. They are on the top branches swaying about dangerously, crying and shivering.

I rushed into the house and begged my vati to do something. I said, "They might fall off and die."

And he said, "Good."

6:00 p.m.

Eventually the fire brigade were called. You have never seen anything as embarrassing as my mother. She was practically dribbling as the "boys", as she called the firemen, got their ladders out. She was giggling and saying really stupid things like, "Oh, you must have quite strong arms to hold those big hoses." I was looking at her, but she ignored me.

In the end she accidentally phoned up her aerobics mates and they all came round to watch the "boys" as well, giggling like a bunch of giggling Gerties. It is soooo shaming.

6:25 p.m.
"Ben", Mum's new fireman friend, got to the top of the ladder to try to grab the kittykats to safety. He was reaching out from his big ladder with a net thing, and as he reached out to them Angus and Gordy stopped shivering and yowling and just scampered merrily down the tree and off into the undergrowth.

Unbelievable.

They are the devil incarnate in furry trousers.

They had been toying with the firemen.

Monday July 11th
Jas had already gone to Stalag 14 when I arrived at her gate.

Assembly

And she stood at the other end of the Ace Gang, not in her usual place next to me.

How long can she keep this up?

This is marathon *ignorez-vous*ing.

French

I snuggled up really close to her, but she shifted her chair further and further away from me until she was practically sitting on Ellen's knee.

P.E.

I said to her, "I like your pants today, Jas."

She still had her Huffy Pants on though.

Ace Gang Headquarters

The Ace Gang have been on at me all day to sing and the world sings with you. They want to go to the Stiff Dylans gig on Saturday, and they say they can't go unless I go because it will not be one for all and all for one. Also, Rosie is having a practice of her Viking wedding at the gig. She wants to dress up and try out the Viking bison dance.

♥ 237

She's got the confetti but fortunately not the vats.

They tried to bribe me with cheesy snacks, which is pathetic.

When I say "they", I don't mean Jas, who is still giving me the cold shoulder. This is a world record for her. Four days. I said to her, "Jas, are you going to eschew me with a firm hand for ever?"

She didn't say anything.

Rosie was going, "Come on, Gee, please come to the gig, pleasey please and double please with knobs. Please don't spoil my big day. You only get married to a Viking and madman once in your life. And anyway, what else will you be doing? Crying, that's what."

Jools said, "There might be some really cool boys there."

I said, "Look, Masimo will be there wanting to be my 'mate' and Dave the Laugh will be with stupid old Emma thingy and..."

Uh-oh. Ellen started: "What do you mean Dave the Laugh will be with Emma? Why are you, like, er, bothered by that? I mean has, er..."

Jas said, "Yeah, what do you mean about Dave the Laugh?"

I fell to my knees. "She speaks, it's a miracle, she can speak!!! The good Lord has given her back the power of speech."

Hahahahah. She couldn't go back on it; she had asked me a question. She had broken her vow of cold shoulderosity. I won, I won!!! (And distracted Ellen from the Dave the Laugh fandango.)

But I was magnaniwhatsit in victory. "I love you, Jazzy, and I'm sorry about the ditch incident. But you were being vair vair annoying, my little pally."

She humped around, but she was sick of not talking to me.

1:30 p.m.
I've said I might go to the Stiff Dylans gig. But if I do the Ace Gang has got to look after me like little guardey dogs. I said that, "If you leave me on my own while you all go off snogging, I will resign from the Ace Gang."

Rosie said, "This will be a magnificent evening. We will wear our newly liberated horns and show the world that romance lives."

I said, "Er, I don't think we need to bother with the

horns. I mean, why don't we just keep them for private moments that—"

Rosie said, "Aren't you proud to wear your horns?"

"Yes, of course, but—"

Rosie put her face very close to mine. "HOOOORRRRN NN!!"

Oh dear God.

We made a solemn Ace Gang vow, and did a quick rendition of the Viking disco inferno dance – with horns. We have also officially added in Jas's sniffing bit. Jas looked all thrilled.

As we huddly-duddlyed down to the floor for the final cry of "Hooorrrrn!!!" Wet Lindsay came by on rounding-up duty. Her extensions are growing out. Hmm, that's attractive. Not. She looked at us; we looked up. Her legs are getting thinner, I swear. Perhaps she is on a leg-thinning diet.

She said, "Get up, you idiots. You're a bloody disgrace, the whole lot of you."

That's charming language, isn't it?

She watched us as we went past her. I was last and she said to me quite quietly, "Don't think I don't know all about you. You're a pathetic, snivelling idiot."

Oh Blimey O'Reilly's trousers she does mean me!!!

German

Wrote a note to Ro Ro: What if Wet Lindsay is still seeing Masimo? And she might be because she has no pridenosity. What if she is with him at the Stiff Dylans gig? I couldn't handle that.

Ro Ro wrote back: One for all and all for one. We will think of a tactic if she is with him, but she won't be. He said that he didn't want to get serious with anyone. And besides — Hooooorrrrrrnnnn!!!

What is she talking about?

Should I go or not?

On the way home

Jas and me are besties again. Jas was still rambling on about the hidden depths she had found out about herself as Lady MacUseless, and Rosie was practising burping, when we saw the titchey first formers hopping along in front of us.

When we caught up with them, I said to one of the titches, "What are you doing?"

She was wheezing and red but managed to say, "Er, we're hopping, miss."

Miss?

I said, "I can see that, but why?"

And she said, "I don't know."

How mad is that?

Rosie was looking at them. "I wonder if they are related to Sven?"

Wednesday July 13th

Still can't decide whether to go to the gig or not.

I'm glad that Jas and I are pals again. She gave me two Midget Gems and a Jammy Dodger, which I have to say is nice. Even though she is vair vair annoying, I love her really, but not, you know, in a lezzie way.

4:10 p.m.

Walking home on my own. Which is unusual. Jas has gone off with Tom on a foraging expedition and the rest have gone into town on a make-up shopping spree. I wasn't in the mood somehow. No sign of Dave and his mates, either.

I am indeed Georgia Nomates.

Ah, well, that is the harsh truth of life in a cake shop of ag... Is that the littlies hopping again?

Surely not?

One minute later
It is, though. They are hopping like loons into the park.

One minute later
And there's Mark Big Gob and the Blunder Boys. What are the hoppers doing hanging around them? I sincerely hope they're not going for snogging lessons. Erlack apongo. If Mark Big Gob kisses one of them, they will be eaten alive. I know he likes tee-tiny girls, but this is ridiculous.

What is going on?

The girls are handing something over to Mark, still hopping.

One minute later
The Blunder Boys are all laughing and smoking as the titches hop off.

Three minutes later
I caught up with the hoppers, who were lying down on the

grass behind a bush. I said, "Oy, what are you doing?"

One of them said, "Nothing. Just having a lie down."

And the other titch said, "Because we're tired from hopping."

I said, "I can see that. But WHY? Are you a bit half-witted? And what were you doing with Mark and his mates?"

They were redder than red things at a red convention.

Half an hour later

It turns out that they're being tormented by Mark and his mates. They make the little titches hand over their lunch money and any sweet money they have, and if they haven't got any spondulies, the gang make them hop home. And they keep making surprise appearances so that the titches never know when to stop hopping.

What is the matter with Mark and his mates? Haven't they got anything better to do? I thought the day would never come when I would say this, but they are worse than the Bummer twins in their heyday.

In bed

I keep thinking about the stupid little hoppers.

Midnight
What if it was Bibbsy being made to hop?

12:10 a.m.
Yeah, as if. I'd like to see the boy who could make her do anything.

12:15 a.m.
But the little titches are such weedy blubbers.

12:30 a.m.
Oh blimey, I'm going to have to save them.

Thursday July 14th
At break I found the titches and said, "Your hopping days are over."

In the park
4:30 p.m.
Mark Big Gob and the Blunder Boys were louting about, waiting for their hopping victims.

The little titches hid behind a bush while I went up to see the lard arses.

5:00 p.m.

After they had stopped leering at my nungas, I said to Oscar, "OK, Perv Boy, I'm going to tell your mum you smoke, and then you'll be a dead Perv Boy."

The other Blunder Boys started sniggering, and I said to them, "if you don't back off, I'm going to spread the word at school that you've all got infectious warts. No girl will ever snog you again. That is a fact."

5:30 p.m.

The titches followed me all the way to my gate. They were saying, "Thanks, Georgia. Would you like some Midget Gems, Georgia? What's your favourite colour? Which band do you like best, Georgia?"

Good grief.

I don't want any tiny hopping pals.

7:00 p.m.

Still don't know whether to go to the gig or not.

I feel like I haven't snogged anyone for years.

Do you know why that is? Because I haven't snogged anyone for years.

The last time was when I saw Dave, and that was snoggus interruptus at Katie's. Two weeks ago.

Who do I think is the best snogger between Masimo and Dave?

Well, Masimo, obviously, as he is the Luuurve God. And he did that neck-nuzzling thing that was mega-groovy and even thinking about it makes my legs go jelloid.

Not to mention my brain.

7:40 p.m.

On the other hand, Dave is the king of nip libbling.

I wonder if boys mark girls out of ten for snogging like we do?

I must ask Dave.

No, I'd better not. He has a way of knowing what I'm thinking about and he would know that I was thinking about him.

Friday July 15th
10:00 a.m.
When I walked past Slim's headquarters today, I noticed the school photo had been put up. I stopped to look at it because I wanted to know if you could see the beauty spots the Ace Gang had all pencilled in on our top lips, especially for the photo.

One minute later
Ahaha. Yep, you had to look really closely, but there they were. The revolution starts here!!! Since the piggy-nose scenario last year, when our clearly hilarious joke of making little pig noses out of egg carton bits had resulted in mass bad-conduct marks and *ordure*, we had aimed for subtlenosity. And the photo was up and no one had noticed!

One minute later
God, what a bunch of losers the sixth form are. Look at the state of ADM's sad cardigan. And she's next to Miss Slimebum Octopussyhead, Wet Lindsay. And that is when I noticed – Wet Lindsay had a small Hitler moustache pencilled in on her upper lip!!! This was the hand of God at his most amusing.

I was so so excited and happy.

It was a sign – a cosmic sign!

Lunchtime

I told the Ace Gang about the photo and we did a triumphant Viking disco dance. Rosie said, "Let's go and have a look."

And I said, "No, we must display casualosity. If we all troop up and look at the photo, someone will see us and then they'll look and the finger of shame will point our way. Even though, sadly, we are not guilty."

Ellen said, "I wonder who did do it?"

Jools said, "Who really dislikes her?"

And I said, "No, Jools, the question is, who DOESN'T dislike her?"

Walking home

The whole Ace Gang has verified that in fact Wet Lindsay is now officially a member of the Hitler Youth.

I said, "If Miss Stamp sees her moustache, it will be love at first sight."

5:00 p.m.

As I went round the corner from the bottom road into my street, I caught sight of two little heads bobbing along behind me. It was the hopping titches. Oh good grief, now I was even a "mate" of first formers. Still, I stopped and they caught up with me. Ginger Titch said, "Did you think Wet Lindsay's moustache was funny?"

I looked at them and they looked all proud of themselves.

I said, "Yeah, it was brillopads, but how do you know about it?"

They giggled and said, "We did it for you, miss."

Hells bells. They love me and think I have saved them. I have turned into a combination of Superman and Jesus – not that Jesus would wear tights.

Saturday July 16th

11:00 a.m.

Jas on the phone in a pants frenzy. "Gee. Ooooooohhhhh."

"What? What?"

"Oh, this is so exciting!!!"

"Have you discovered a new kind of slug?"

"No."

"New panties that go right up to your neck?"

"No... oooh, I wish I could tell you."

"Let me get this right, Jas, you have rung me up to tell me something that you can't tell me, is that it?"

"Yeah!!!"

"Goodbye, then. Thanks."

I put the phone down.

Jas on the phone
Thirty seconds later

"I'll tell you a bit then."

I waited. Oh, the tensionosity. Not. It will be something so boring about Jas's life. If she tells me that she and Hunky are going to have a double wedding with Rosie and Sven, I may lose what little mind I have got left. She's bound to want to have a woodland wedding. We'll all have to dress as elves and huddle on twigs and...

Jas was rambling on: "Tom says if you come to the gig tonight, you're in for a big surprise."

I said, "Why? Has it been cancelled?"

"Noooo... oooh, I wish I could tell you, but I promised. Oh, it's so... oh, well, anyway, you've got to come now, please, will you? Please come."

"Say, 'Please will you come, I love you, you are my besty.'"

There was a pause. I said, "Don't you want me to come?"

She said, "Er, well... Please will you come, I love you, you are my besty."

I said, "I will think about it. Goodbye."

Yessssssssss!!! I win hahahaha. Jazzy Spazzy had to say she luuurved me. Teehee.

I'm definitely not going now.

3:00 p.m.

I've decided again to go to the gig. Partly to get out of the house because Grandvati is coming round tonight. And I am a bit interested in what Tom has to say. I mean, if it was just Jas that was saying I should go, I would be a bit suspicious because her idea of "exciting" and "good" are different to mine. But Tom is, on the whole, not entirely mad for a boy.

4:00 p.m.

I wonder what it could be? I wonder if he's spoken to Masimo? He did say that he'd try to find out stuff for me. Maybe Masimo has told him that the "mates" thing was a mistake.

5:00 P.M.

What on earth shall I wear?

6:30 P.M.

Grandvati turned up in his "leisure" wear. Is it normal for octogenarians to wear tartan zoot suits? With matching cap? And blusher?

I went downstairs to say hello, even though I am vair vair busy trying to find something to wear for the gig. He was in the front room giving Libby the bumps. I waved to him and he waved back and smiled. He hasn't got his teeth in. I said to Mum, "Mum, my venerated grandfather is wearing make-up."

She just turned her eyes skyward and said, "Don't start me off. They say women go through a funny patch as they get older, but they're practically saints compared to men. He says he's taking up waterskiing."

I said, "Will he be wearing a wet suit?"

She said, "I'm afraid so."

Good grief.

After Grandvati had given me the usual ten pence to "get something nice for yourself". (Like what? Half a stamp?) I went back to my boudoir.

♡ 253

There must be something perfect for me to wear that will have Masimo desperate not to be my mate.

7:00 p.m.
Ready at last. I finally decided on my pleated kilt, boots and cross-over top. I went downstairs hoping to nip out of the door without a Nazi interrogation from Vati, but sadly he was just emerging from collecting extra pie rations from the kitchen. He looked me up and down. "Er, I think you'll find that you've forgotten to put a skirt on, Georgia."

Oh, vair vair *amusant*.

Mum came out of the kitchen with a struggling Gordy and chucked him outside and banged the door. He was howling and then started hurling himself against the door. Mum went into the front room and said, "Libby, you must not put him in the fridge any more."

"He laaaikes it."

"I know he likes it. He was lying in the butter. It's disgusting."

Vati was still raving on about my skirt. "Have you seen this, Connie? Look at the state she thinks she's going out in. You can practically see what she had for her tea."

What is he talking about? And also, that's a laugh, what I had for tea. I didn't have anything for "tea". We don't have stuff for tea.

Mum said, "Oh, for goodness' sake, Bob, it's fashion. They all look stupid; it's not just her."

Oh, very supportive coming from someone who's wearing a top so tight that her nungas are practically extra arms. But I didn't say that because I saw a window of opportunity for an escape while they argued the toss about fashion and so on.

Vati was still going on: "Oh, so it's all right that she looks like a prostitute because it's fashion? I suppose if leather bikinis were fashion you wouldn't mind your teenage daughter going out in one?"

Mum said, "You're being stupid, Bob. Leather bikinis will never be the fashion."

Grandad said, "Leather bikinis not fashionable? You tell Maisie and the rest of the lasses at the Housing Association that!"

I can't begin to let that image into my brain. On the plus side, it did stun Dad so much that I was able to get through the door and escape.

Clock tower

I had forgotten for a minute how nervy I am. I am sure I'm having a heart attack; my heart is plip-plopping and racing. I must get a grip. This is going to be the ultimate glaciosity test.

Jas, Ellen, Mabs and Jools were all at the clock tower. We did our special Klingon salute. Jas was being very annoying coming up to me and hugging me and going, "Oooohhhhhhhh, I am soooooo excited."

If it's anything to do with any form of livestock, this "exciting" thing that she is so excited about, I will have to simply and quietly put her out of her misery. A glancing blow to the head should do it.

We started walking to the gig. I said, "Where are Ro Ro and Sven?"

Mabs said, "The bride and bridegroom phoned and said they'd see us there."

Fifteen minutes later

I feel like every footstep is bringing me closer to my fate. I don't know what I expect, anyway. He has said he wants to be my mate; that's the end of the story. Maybe there will be someone else there that I like. Yeah, whatever.

In the tarts' wardrobe

Ironically, for once my hair is not buggering about and there are no lurking lurker incidents. I decided against wearing the boy entrancers. At first I thought I'd do a double bluff on Our Lord. I thought I wouldn't wear them because I might end up in a snogging scenario and they might come adrift with tragic consequences. But then I thought I SHOULD wear them because that would imply I didn't think that there'd be snogging action and God would think that was sad, and then He would give me a surprise by giving me snogging action. But then I thought that He knows our every thought, even when we are on the lavatory, so He would know I was doing double bluffsies. So in the end what it comes down to is what sort of mood Our Lord is in. I should tell Call-me-Arnold to put that in his sermon if he wants to depress people. If God is in a smiting mood He will smite away to His heart's content, and if He is in a peachy mood, it also didn't matter what I was wearing.

In the end, I couldn't get the entrancers on straight, and after I had stabbed myself in the eye with my mascara, I called it a day entrancerwise.

Still, I had done a good job on the old layering of the

mascara, and my lippy was good. It looked all poutey pout and so on. I was just inspecting myself from the side, smiling and looking confident, when Jas came out of the loo.

"Why are you doing an impression of a goldfish? Are you fishing for compliments? Or are you trying to look NETural?!" And she went cackling off. She really does imagine that she's funny. Also, she did that weird hugging thing again and also said, "Wrrrrrrrr."

Why?

8:30 p.m.
The Stiff Dylans are on in a minute. I am on piddly-diddly duty about every two minutes.

8:35 p.m.
It's rammed in the club. I couldn't see Dave the Laugh and his mates. Perhaps they weren't coming. No sign of the happy couple. Or Wet Lindsay.

I said to Jas, "Oh dear, no sign of Wet Lindsay. I hope she hasn't fallen down some grating on the way here. That would be tragic. Not."

8:40 p.m.

Then Ellen said, "Oh, look, there's Dave. He looks cool, doesn't he? He, I think, he's like on his own. Can you see Emma? I can't see Emma, can you? Can you see her?"

Ellen might be on my killing list as well as Jas at this rate.

Two minutes later

Tom arrived. He walked in and saw Jas. He did a thumbsie-up to her and she did one back. How sad and uncool is that? They only saw each other about an hour ago. It's pathetico. But quite touching when you're a spinster of the parish. I suppose I should be happy for them. I am, really. But if she hugs me one more time, I will definitely deck her.

Stiff Dylans onstage

My tummy turned over when Masimo walked out onstage. He is just so gorgey. Actually, I don't know why I thought he would like me – he is clearly a ten and as Jas so kindly reminded me, I once got nothing out of ten for my nose. In fact, my average for features was six and a half. Six and a halfs do not go out with tens – that is the law of the snogging jungle.

Half an hour later

The Stiff Dylans rule. They are groove personified.

I know I am wound up on the rack of luuurve and so on but the music is so good everyone has gone mental. The Ace Gang is giving our world-renowned disco inferno exhibition. Everyone except Rosie and Sven, that is. I wonder where they are? Probably snogging in the chip shop. I wish they were here.

Half an hour later

Still dancing. I am showing *joie de vivre* and *savoir faire* to Masimo.

I'm boiling but I don't care. I think a bit of a healthy glow is nice in a girl.

Jas said, "Blimey, you're red. You look like you've plunged your head into a vat of boiling oil."

Oh good. I dashed off to the tarts' wardrobe for a bit of a dampening-down and titivating session.

Back in the club
Five minutes later

Dave and Rollo and Tom came over and joined us in a sort of

semi Viking disco inferno dance. But without the horns; Rosie is in charge of horns. Dave added some moves of his own, although it was a bit of a surprise when he leaped up into my arms. I managed to take his weight for a minute before he leaped down. He does make me laugh. We even did linksie-up disco dancing. Then he went off and he shouted to me, "Off to the piddly-diddly department, and I won't spare the horses!"

As we were doing our dance routines in front of the stage, I like to think that Masimo was looking at me in an admiring way. Either that or that he was thinking, *My new mate has gone mad.*

But I refuse to be sad.

Actually, Masimo did smile at me quite a lot when he caught my eye. But I am not so stupid that I think it means anything. I said to Jas, "Did you see Masimo looking at me?"

She said, "Forget about him; he is yesterday's news."

Thanks.

10:45 p.m.

I was dancing backwards when someone kicked my ankle really viciously. Buggering bums bugger. And also ouch. I looked round and there was Wet Lindsay and Astonishingly

Dim Monica. They must have slimed in while I wasn't looking. They were doing exceptionally crap dancing with their other crap mates from Crap City.

I said to Lindsay, "Oy."

And she came up to me, still smiling in a really scary way, and said, "Oh dear, you danced into my foot."

And then she waved at Masimo, who annoyingly nodded back and smiled.

Jas said, "Boy, does she hate you. You are dead meat. You live in Dead Meat City."

Cheers, thanks a lot. Hurrah another two happy years of Stalag 14 with a sadistic stick insect who hates me. I'll be lucky to come out of school fully limbed.

Five minutes later

The Stiff Dylans are on a break.

I am in a complete ditherspaz as to how to handle the situation. I can't just be hanging around, looking like goosegog of the century, when Masimo comes offstage. I know what I'll do: I'll go and talk to Dave the Laugh, that'll be cool. Also it will get me away from Jas and Tom, who seem to have lost their marbles. They keep looking at me and going into huddles and laughing like excited newts. Still no sign of Ro Ro and Sven.

I went over to the bar where I had last seen Dave. There he was, leaning against it, talking to his mates. Perfect. I was just about to go up to him when Emma appeared. Dave had his back to me, so he couldn't see me, and Emma came up to him and kissed him on the cheek. And then in front of everyone he put his arms round her and gave her a proper snog. No mistaking it. Not just a cheeksie, but proper lip-on-lip action. I felt really sick to my stomach. When he eventually stopped kissing her, he put his arm around her waist and bought her a drink. It was like they were proper boyfriend and girlfriend. I was so shocked.

I turned to go to the tarts' wardrobe, and as I did Masimo came out of the dressing room. He saw me and smiled and started to walk over to me. Oh God, what should I do? What would a mate do? Smack him on the shoulder when he came over and do the Klingon salute? I don't know, I don't know. I've never done mates with boys before.

There was only one thing for it. I looked at my watch and then looked surprised, slapped my head in the manner of someone who has forgotten an appointment, and then quickly walked to the tarts' wardrobe.

In the tarts' wardrobe

I'll tell you why I looked surprised when I looked at my watch, shall I? I haven't got a watch, that's why.

One minute later

Also, what sort of person has an appointment in the tarts' wardrobe? An idiot, that's what kind of person.

A sad twat.

Me.

One minute later

I sat down on the loo with my head in my hands. What could be worse than this?

Jas and Mabs and Ellen came to find me. I told them what had happened. Jas said, "Oh, well, maybe something really NICE will happen."

I said, "Yeah and maybe Hitler was really lovable, just misunderstood."

Mabs said, "Er, I think there's something else you should know."

Oh yeah, like what? I've been going round all night with my skirt stuck in my knickers?

I said, "Go on, then, what else could be worse than what is already happening? Oh, I know, Wet Lindsay is with Masimo."

At that point, Lindsay stormed into the tarts' wardrobe with Monica trailing behind her. Lindsay was all red-faced and flustered and looked like she was going to cry. So there is a silver lining to every cloud.

Not. Because she was saying to Monners, "How could Masimo just turn up with some Italian bint? How could he?"

They went down the other end of the loos when they saw us.

I looked at Mabs. She said, "Ah, well, yes, the other thing you should know."

In the club

I had to see the full fiasco with my own peepers. Masimo was sitting at a table by the side of the stage and leaning in very close to one of the most lovely girls I have ever seen. I don't say that because I want to, but she was – she was just

♡ 265

lovely. She might even be a ten and a half.

Word must have spread on the Radio Jas airwaves because Ellen came scuttling over and Jools and all of the gang. I must not cry.

Ellen said, "I just, you know, like, casually walked by and they are speaking in Pizza-a-gogo language."

I was frozen to the spot and couldn't help looking at them. Masimo put his hand up to the Italian girl's face and pushed back her hair.

I must go home.

I glanced across the room because I felt like everyone must know what a fool I was. I could see Dave the Laugh sitting at the bar with Emma. She was talking to Rollo and Dave had his arm round her. I don't know why, but he suddenly looked round and straight at me. Then he looked at where Masimo was sitting with the Italian girl. He said something to Emma and kissed her cheek. Oh good, more and more agony.

I must get out of here. I said that to Jas, "I'm going to go home now, Jas. I can't stand this."

She said, "No, no, please don't go. Er... maybe something good will sort of happen."

I looked at her. "Like what, Jas? The sprinkler system might go off?"

As I said that, I saw Wet Lindsay grabbing her coat and storming off into the night. She stropped past the table Masimo was sitting at, but he didn't even notice; he was still talking earnestly to his girlfriend. What a top night this was turning out to be.

I said to the gang, "Well, I can't remember the last time I had so much fun. I think it was when I had to be rushed to hospital with scarlet fever. I'm going to have to go."

As I went off for my coat, Dave the Laugh appeared. "Oh dear, Kittykat, what am I going to do with you?"

I just looked at him, and my eyes filled with tears. He put his arm around me and I so wanted to just have him look after me.

But he had Emma, so I pulled myself together(ish). I must gird my loins with a firm hand. Remember my proud nautical heritage and the Bird of Avon's example. As Sir Billy Shakespeare said in times of stress, "She'll be coming round the mountain when she comes."

I stepped back from Dave and then I heard a voice behind me say, "HOOOORRRN! Oh *jah*, HOOOORRRRRRN!!!"

Tarts' wardrobe

I was sitting on the loo AGAIN with my head in my hands (I practically live in here) when Rosie's horns appeared under the door. Ro Ro said, "Why did you just run off like that?"

I replied, "Well, you're used to Sven."

Ro Ro said, "Good point, but what does that have to do with anything?"

"Well, I was startled by his furry shorts."

Back in the club

Dave and his mates were gathered around Sven, admiring his shorts. The shorts were made out of bits of theatrical fur and a pair of old Y-fronts. Sven had completed his outfit with the bison horns and furry Doc Marten's. And, uh... that was it!

Rosie was wearing a leather skirt and a sort of metallic-looking nunga-nunga holder made out of pan lids.

I said to her, "Why have you got one huge eyebrow?"

And she said, "This is a well known Viking bridal outfit. Get your horns on!"

As Rosie shoved the horns on my head, Masimo appeared in front of me!!!

268

He looked at the horns and, after a few moments of gazing at them, he said a bit nervously, "*Scusi*, Georgia, may I speak with you?"

Oh great, now I was wearing horns and I was going to have to be mates with Masimo while he told me about his new girlfriend.

Dave looked at me a bit weirdly (who wouldn't?) and then he said, "I'll be around if you need me." And he went back to the bar.

Oh noooo, I was on my own. I only had my own brain to help me. God help us one and all. Oh noooo, Masimo was so lovely. His eyes were golden and soft and melty. Booo, no melty eyes, no melty eyes.

And then I remembered I was still wearing the horns. I took them off and looked at them as if I'd never seen them before. I said, "Good heavens, how did they get there?" and flung them on the floor.

He said, "Will you come outside with me, for a little chat?"

No. No. No chatting. No mates just chatting. No.

Perhaps he meant him and his girlfriend. Perhaps he wanted me to be mates with her as well. I couldn't see her

♡ 269

anywhere, but she might come popping up any minute wanting to be mates. I am not putting myself through any more humiliation. I am just going to say, "No, I will not go outside with you, mate."

But of course I followed him outside like a suckling pig. Oh no, I mean a sacrificial lamb. There was no sign of the Italian bint. She was probably at home cooking up some pasta for when he got back from being with his horn-wearing "mates". The Ace Gang were all watching me trail after the Luuurve God. Other girls were looking daggers at me; they needn't bother.

Outside, it was a lovely night. Oh good, and all the stars were out hanging about waiting to see the next exciting instalment in the Georgia is a Prat saga.

Masimo leaned against the wall and looked at me. Please don't look at me like that, it's heartbreaking. Then he said, "Can I to explain things? Gina has come from Italy. She is... er, was my girlfriend, I tell you about. The one I have serious love with, and then we break up, and I... well, I say to you that I want nothing serious."

Yes, yes, I have been to this particular cake shop of aggers before. I didn't know what to say, so I thought I might as well practise my mate skills. Big breath, relax, casualosity and matiness at all times and, "Did you see the footie scores this arvie?"

He looked at me as if I was bonkers.

I am.

Then he laughed. "The footie scores?"

I nodded in an interested way.

He said, "Georgia, Gina has come to see me to tell me she has a new boyfriend."

Pardon?

He was still looking at me. "She was very, you know, had her heart breaking after us, so I felt well... hard for her, hard for me to have a girlfriend. Now she tell me she is better. So all is good."

Is it? What's going on now?

He was still looking at me.

"So, Signorína Georgia, what do you think? Now I am free man for you. If you still want for us to go out."

I was doing my very interesting and world-renowned impression of a goldfish with learning disorders when Jas and Tom appeared at the doorway, beside themselves with excitement.

What is the matter with them? And why are they bothering me now when I practically have a Luuurve God in my hand.

A car pulled up behind me and I heard the car door open and then slam. I was too paralysed to do anything, and besides, I felt like I was in a slow-motion movie.

Masimo was staring over my shoulder. He looked really surprised and said, "*Ciao*. But when did you get back?"

I turned round, and getting out of the car was Robbie.

Robbie.

Robbie whose name I wasn't going to mention this side of the grave.

Robbie who was in Kiwi-a-gogo land.

Playing guitars in streams.

And snogging marsupials.

Except he wasn't.

He was here.

I was quite literally speechless.

The Sex God had re-landed.

Georgia's Glossary

aggers · Agony. Like I said, no one has the time to say whole words, so aggers is short for agony. The unusually irritating among you might point out that aggers is actually longer than agony. My answer to that is – haven't you got something else to do besides count letters?

Alsatian · This is a big wolfy-type guard doggie, so called because it is from Alsatia, that well known place in, erm... Lederhosen land. Possibly. Oh, I don't know. Why am I being bothered with this? I am vair vair tired, and it's only a dog when all is said and done.

arvie · Afternoon. From the Latin "arvo". Possibly. As in the famous Latin invitation: "Lettus meetus this arvo."

balaclava · This is from the Crimean War when our great-great-grannies spent all their time knitting hats to keep the English soldiers warm in the very, very cold Baltic. A balaclava covers everything apart from your eyes. It's like a big sock with a hole in it. Which just goes to show what really crap knitters our great-great-grannies were.

bhaji · A bhaji is an Indian food. An onion bhaji is brown and round and full of fat, hence my hilarious joke about Slim looking like one. I exhaust myself with my good humour, I really do.

billio · From the Australian outback. A billycan was something Aborigines boiled their goolies up in, or whatever it is they eat. Anyway, billio means boiling things up. Therefore, "my cheeks ached like billio" means, er... very achy. I don't know why we say it. It's a mystery, like many things. But that's the beauty of life.

Blimey O'Reilly · (as in "Blimey O'Reilly's trousers") This is an Irish expression of disbelief and shock. Maybe Blimey O'Reilly was a famous Irish bloke who had extravagantly big trousers. We may never know the truth. The fact is, whoever he is, what you need to know is that a) it's Irish and b) it is Irish. I rest my case.

Boboland · As I have explained many, many times, English is a lovely and exciting language full of sophisticosity. To go to sleep is "to go to bobos", so if you go to bed you are going to Boboland. It is an Elizabethan expression. (Oh, OK then, Libby made it up and she can be unreasonably violent if you don't join in with her.)

boy entrancers · Ah, yes, the re-emergence of the boy entrancers. Hmmm... well... boy entrancers are false eyelashes. They are known as boy entrancers because they entrance boys. Normally. However, I've had some non-entrancing moments with them. For instance, the time I used too much glue to stick them on with. It was when I was at a Stiff Dylans gig trying to entrance Masimo. I was intending to do that looking up at him and then looking down and then looking up again thing, and possibly a bit of flicky hair (as suggested in *How to Make Any Twit Fall in Love with You*). I did the looking at him and looking down thing, but when I tried to look up again I couldn't because my BEs had stuck to my bottom lashes. So my eyes stayed shut. I tried raising my eyebrows (that must have looked good) and humming, but in the end, out of sheer desperadoes, I said,

"Oooh, I love this one..." and went off doing blind disco-dancing to Rolf Harris's "Two Little Boys". So, in conclusion, boy entrancers are good, but be alert for glue extravaganzas.

bugger · A swear word. It doesn't really mean anything but neither do a lot of swear words. Or parents.

bum-oley · Quite literally bottom hole. I'm sorry but you did ask. Say it proudly (with a cheery smile and a Spanish accent).

chav · A chav is a common rude rough person. They wear naff clothes. A chav joke would be, "What are the first words a chav baby says to its single parent?" Answer: "What are YOU looking at?" Or: "If there are two chavs in a car and no loud music playing, what kind of a car is it?" Answer: "A police car."

Chingachgook · He was the last of the Mohicans. He hung around with Davy Crockett and they both wore hats made out of old beavers. (They were dead, the beavers, not just old and having a little doze on Davy and Chingachgook's heads.)

chuddie · Chewing gum. This is an "i" word thing. We have a lot of them in English due to our very busy lives explaining stuff to other people not so fortunate as ourselves.

clud · This is short for cloud. Lots of really long boring poems and so on can be made much snappier by abbreviating words. So Wordsworth's poem called "Daffodils" (or "Daffs") has the immortal line "I wandered lonely as a clud". Ditto *Rom and Jul* or *Ham* or *Merc of Ven*.

conk · Nose. This is very interesting historically. A very long time ago (1066) – even before my grandad was born – a bloke called William the Conqueror (French) came to England and shot our King Harold in the eye. Typical. And people wonder why we don't like the French much. Anyway, William had a big nose and so to get our own back we called him William the Big Conk-erer. If you see what I mean. I hope you do because I am exhausting myself with my hilariosity and historiosity.

div · Short for "dithering prat", i.e., Jas.

double cool with knobs · "Double" and "with knobs" are instead of saying very or very, very, very, very. You'd feel silly saying, "He was very, very, very, very, very cool". Also everyone would have fallen asleep before you had finished your sentence. So "double cool with knobs" is altogether snappier.

duffing up · Duffing up is the female equivalent of beating up. It is not so violent and usually involves a lot of pushing with the occasional pinch.

fandango · A fandango is a complicated Spanish dance. So a fandango is a complicated thing. Yes, I know there is no dancing involved. Or Spanish.

fives court · This is a typical Stalag 14 idea. It's minus forty-five degrees outside so what should we do to entertain the schoolgirls? Let them stay inside in the cosy warmth and read? No, let's build a concrete wall outside with a red line at waist height and let's make them go and hit a hard ball at the red line with their little freezing hands. What larks!

froggie and geoggers · Froggie is short for French,

geoggers is short for geography. Ditto blodge (biology) and lunck (lunch).

f.t. · I refer you to the famous "losing it" scale:
minor tizz
complete tizz and to do
strop
a visit to Strop Central
f.t. (funny turn)
spaz attack
complete ditherspaz
nervy b. (nervous breakdown)
complete nervy b.
ballisticisimus

goosegog · Gooseberry. I know you are looking all quizzical now. OK. If there are two people and they want to snog and you keep hanging about saying, "Do you fancy some chewing gum?" or "Have you seen my interesting new socks?" you are a gooseberry. Or for short a goosegog, i.e., someone who nobody wants around.

gorgey · Gorgeous. Like fabby (fabulous) and marvy (marvellous).

havvies · Haversacks. Life is too shor to fini wor...

Horn · When you "have the Horn" it's the same as "having the big red bottom".

Jammy Dodger · Biscuit with jam in it. Very nutritious(ish).

jimjams · Pyjamas. Also pygmies or jammies.

joggerbums · Trousers that you jog in. Jogging trousers.

Kiwi-a-gogo land · New Zealand. "a-gogo land" can be used to liven up the otherwise really boring names of other countries. America, for instance, is Hamburger-a-gogo land, Mexico is Mariachi-a-gogo land and France is Frogs'-legs-a-gogo land. Masimo comes from Pizza-a-gogo land – land of wine, sun, olives and vair vair groovy Luuurve Gods. Otherwise known as Italy. (The only bad point about Pizza-a-gogo land is their football players are so vain that if it rains, they all run off the pitch so that their hair doesn't get ruined. See also Chelsea players.)

Late and Live · A late-night gig which has live bands on.

Manchester United · An English football team from the north of England, otherwise known as "The Scum". The most hated team apart from "The Blue Scum" (Chelsea). There is an important difference between them – one wears a red strip and the other wears blue. That is all you need to know.

Midget Gem · Little sweets made out of hard jelly stuff in different fruit flavours. Jas loves them A LOT. She secretes them about her person, I suspect, often in her knickers, so I never like to accept one from her on hygiene and lesbian grounds.

mug's game · As in "love is a mug's game". The beauty of Billy Shakespeare language is that it is multi whatsit. For instance "mug" can mean a cup. However, even the very dim amongst you (and I mean that in a caring way) can see that saying "love is a cup's game" is just silly. A mug can also mean a face. However "love is a face's game" doesn't have *je ne sais quoi* and verve. And this is where we come to my nub – mug can also mean a "fool", like for instance my vati. So there you have it. "Love is a fool's game." Which is *le* fact.

nippy noodles · Instead of saying, "Good heavens, it's quite cold this morning," you say "Cor – nippy noodles!!" English is an exciting and growing language. It is. Believe me. Just leave it at that. Accept it.

nuddy-pants · Quite literally nude-coloured pants, and you know what nude-coloured pants are? They are no pants. So if you are in your nuddy-pants, you are in your no pants, i.e., you are naked.

nunga-nungas · Basoomas. Girls' breasty business. Ellen's brother calls them nunga-nungas because he says that if you get hold of a girl's breast and pull it out and then let it go, it goes nunga-nunga-nunga. As I have said many, many times with great wisdomosity, there is something really wrong with boys.

Pacamac · A rainproof coat that folds up into a tiny packet that you can pop in your handbag. It keeps you dry but you look like a fool.

Pantalitzer · A terrifying Czech-made doll that sadistic parents (my vati) buy for their children, presumably to teach them early on about the horror of life. Essentially the Pantalitzer doll has a weird plastic face with a horrible fixed smile. The rest of Pantalitzer is a sort of cloth bag with hard plastic hands on each side like steel forks. I don't know if I have mentioned this before, but I am not reassured that Eastern Europeans really know how to have a laugh.

Pavlov's dogs · Pavlov was some Russian bloke who had some dogs. He trained them to dribble when he rang a bell. Don't ask me why. The Russians are, as we all know, a bit on the strange side. Cossack dancing for instance. I rest my case.

red-bottomosity · Having the big red bottom. This is vair vair interesting vis-à-vis nature. When a lady baboon is "in the mood" for luuuurve, she displays her big red bottom to the male baboon. (Apparently he wouldn't have a clue otherwise, but that is boys for you!!) Anyway, if you hear the call of the Horn you are said to be displaying red-bottomosity.

sailor's hornpipe · As I have pointed out many, many times, England is a proud seafaring nation and our sailors on the whole are jolly good chaps etc. However, when they were first invented in the olden days, they had a few too many rums and made up this odd dance called a "hornpipe", which largely consists of hopping from foot to foot with your arms crossed. Well, you did ask.

spangleferkel · A kind of German sausage. I know, you couldn't make it up, could you? The German language is full of this kind of thing, like lederhosen and so on. And *Goosegot*.

squid · Squid is the plural of quid, and I do know why that is: a bloke owed another bloke six pounds, or six quid, and he goes up to him with an octopus with one of its tentacles bandaged up, and he says, "Hello, mate. Here is the sick squid I owe you." Do you see?? Do you see? Sick squid – six quid??? The marvellous juxtaposition of... Look, we just call pounds squids. Leave it at that. Try and get on with it, people.

titches · A titch is a small person. Titches is the plural of titch.

toadying · This is when a person is all slimy and sucky and tries to get stuff by pretending to be nice.

tushy pegs · Tush rhymes with mush, which means face (keep up), so the pegs in your mush are your teeth. Now do you see? Well, just accept it.

vicars and tarts party · A traditional fancy-dress party that "grown-ups" think is hilarious. Everyone goes to the party either dressed up as a vicar or a prostitute. It is sad. What is even sadder though is that I was coming home once and accidentally bumped into Call-me-Arnold the vicar wheeling his sad bike home. I was trying to get away from him when a group of lads came by and said, "Oy, where's the party?" because they thought we were dressed up as a vicar and a tart. Good grief. It's quite bad for someone to think you're dressed up as a tart, but much much worse that they may have thought Call-me-Arnold was my boyfriend.

wally · See prat. A wally additionally has no clothes sense.

Welligogs · Wellington boots. Because it more or less rains all the time in England we have special rubber boots that we wear to keep us above the mud. This is true.

Whelks · A horrible shellfish thing that only the truly mad (like my grandad, for instance) eat. They are unbelievably slimy and mucuslike.

Winceyette · Is like fluffy nylon material, usually pink. If you wear it, it makes your hair stand on end because it's so full of static electricity. The elderly insane LOVE it.

Woad · The Ancient Britons used to dye themselves blue with a plant called woad. I don't know why they didn't like pink as a skin colour. They just preferred to be blue. But that is the Ancient Britons for you.

Womble · Yes. Now, *The Wombles of Wimbledon* was a crap TV show about these creatures who lived in Wimbledon. The wombles were supposed to be giant hamsters but were quite clearly tubby blokes in hairy costumes. They mostly wandered about Wimbledon Common collecting litter. Oh, and they had a number one hit with "Remember You're a Womble". The lyrics were, "Remember you're a womble, remember you're a womble. Remember, member, member, what a womble, womble, womble you are." That is how great the whole thing was.

Woopsie · *Ordure* and *merde*. Ok, have it your way, poo.

Look out for the next instalment of

Georgia's hilarious diary

'Luuurve is a many
trousered thing...'

Available in July 2007
Sound the Cosmic Horn!!!

If you just can't wait till then, visit

www.georgianicolson.com

for exclusive sneaky peeks
at the new book, and while you're there...

- join the Ace Gang
- ♡ download gorgey stuff
- win fabbity-fab prizes
- ♡ vote for your favourite Sex God
- send in photos of your bestest pallies
- ♡ chat to new chums on message boards
- and much, much more!